Loch

The Powers Th

Book 3

Harper Bentley

Check out other titles by Harper Bentley:

The Powers That Be series:

Gable (The Powers That Be Book 1)

Zeke (The Powers That Be Book 2)

CEP series:

Being Chased (CEP #1)

Unbreakable Hearts (CEP #2)

Under the Gun (CEP #3) coming March 2016!

Serenity Point series:

Bigger Than the Sky (Serenity Point Book 1)

Always and Forever (Serenity Point Book 2)

True Love series:

Discovering Us (True Love #1)

Finding Us (True Love #2)

Finally Us (True Love Book 3)

True Love: The Trilogy: The Complete Boxed Set

http://harperbentleywrites.com/

Copyright © 2015 Harper Bentley

CreateSpace Edition: September 2015

Editors: Franca, Mel & Sam

Cover image licensed by www.shutterstock.com

Cover Photo design by Jada D'Lee Designs

All rights reserved.

No part of this book may be reproduced or transmitted in any form or by any means, electronic or mechanical, including photocopying, recording, or by any information storage and retrieval system without the written permission of the author, except for the use of brief quotations in a book review. This book is a work of fiction. Names, characters, places, and incidents either are the products of the author's imagination or are used fictitiously. Any resemblance to actual persons, living or dead, events, or locations is entirely coincidental. All rights reserved. Except as permitted under the U.S. Copyright Act of 1976, no part of this publication may be reproduced, distributed, or transmitted in any form or by any means, or stored in a database or retrieval system, without the prior express, written consent of the author

Dedication

To Sam

Who always makes me

feel WAY better

Even when I'm just bumbling along

YOU'RE the awesome one!

♥

Confession Number One

    I pushed my glasses up my nose and stood watching as the love of my life danced with Misti Fitzgerald, the prettiest, most popular girl in class, and couldn't help the tumble that my heart took at seeing him smile down at her.

    "He's such a jerk!" Marcy Belton, my best friend, hissed as she came and stood beside me at the edge of the gymnasium floor, hands on her hips.

    I couldn't have agreed more but I just shrugged. I mean, what could I do other than stare as Lochlan Powers rocked back and forth to the slow song that was playing with another girl in his arms. A girl who wasn't me. Me, who happened to be his date for the evening.

    When the song finished, I then observed with horror him bending and kissing her... on the mouth! Then he held her hand as he led her off the floor.

    "Oh, my God," Marcy bit out. "I'm gonna let him have it!"

    She grabbed me by the hand and tugged me with her as she crossed the gym floor, cutting through couples and not even excusing herself, to the opposite corner where all the cool sixth graders were hanging out.

    "Marcy! No!" I pleaded, trying to get my hand free from hers, but it was of no use since we'd already arrived at her destination.

    "Loch!" she yelled.

    When he turned to see who was shouting at him, I watched as he regarded us both with annoyed consideration, me especially.

Marcy marched right up and got in his face. "Simone is your date! You shouldn't be hanging out with someone else!" She shot Misti a dirty look who gave her one right back.

Loch looked past Marcy's shoulder at me with cold, disapproving brown eyes which made my face instantly hot. Then I watched in morbid fascination as he brought the side of his mouth up in a smirk and looked back at Marcy.

"I don't date geeks."

The kids standing around him laughed to my complete and utter embarrassment and I looked down in humiliation at my first pair of real high heels that I'd ever owned, so cute with the rounded toe and teardrop cutouts. They were black and looked cute with my black and white polka-dotted dress with the flouncy skirt. Compared to the tight, sexy red dress Misti was wearing, I guess mine was kind of babyish but I loved it.

"Let's go, Marcy," I begged, then bit my lip as I avoided the eyes of my cruel classmates.

"No, Sim! He shouldn't be doing this!"

And that was when Loch had gotten mad (probably pretty embarrassed himself at being called out in front of all his friends) and gone for the throat. "Really wanna know why I'm here with her?" The sneer on his face as he tossed a hand toward me let me know that I completely disgusted him. "My mom made me. She felt sorry for her, so she paid me fifty bucks to bring her."

This got an even bigger laugh from his peers and I wanted to crawl under a rock and die.

"Ah!" I cried out as I sat up in bed, breathing hard.

"Nightmare again?" I heard Marcy holler from the bathroom which was across and down the hall from my bedroom in the cute little house we rented.

I flopped back down on my pillow, scrubbing my eyes with my palms. "Yes," I mumbled wishing she hadn't heard me and pissed off that the stupid dreams were happening again.

"Anxiety from all your repressed emotions!" she responded making me groan. Marcy was now a psychology major and I'd been diagnosed by her at least once a week since my return. Yippee.

"Yeah, yeah," I grumbled as I stared up at my bedroom ceiling.

I was back in Seattle where I'd been born and mostly raised. Marcy and I had been best friends since kindergarten and there was no telling how many hours we'd spent as little girls plotting and planning how when we got older we'd share a fancy apartment, we'd both date the most handsome boys on Hallervan University's campus (we'd chosen Hallervan since our parents had gone there and it was smaller than UDub) and we'd both major in veterinary science so we could play with puppies and kittens all day long. But right before my seventh grade year, we'd been devastated when my dad had been transferred to Silicon Valley. And there went our dream.

My older brother Tristan and I had finished school in Palo Alto. Tristan hadn't been happy about the move since it had been his senior year, which I couldn't say I blamed him, and he remained angry the entire year at the fact that he'd had to leave his girlfriend and all his friends behind in Seattle. A week after he graduated, he'd packed up all his things and moved back. Our parents hadn't been thrilled that he'd left so brashly, but they'd understood to a certain extent. When he'd enrolled at UDub that fall, though, all seemed to be forgiven.

After I graduated high school, I'd gone on to attend UC Berkeley the past two years. Marcy and I had stayed in touch since I'd moved then last spring she'd called saying her roommate had moved out, that it would be the perfect time for me to transfer and I'd jumped at the chance. When I'd told my parents, they'd reacted about the same way they had with Tristan just not as emphatically since I was leaving on good terms.

Their apprehension at my leaving was understandable since I was the baby and Berkeley had only been about thirty minutes away, so I'd come home almost every weekend to see them. But I was going to be twenty-one next month and I felt it was time for me to spread my wings.

So, yep, here I was, back in Seattle.

And that's when the nightmares had started again.

Don't get me wrong. I was ecstatic that Marcy and my dream of living together and going to Hallervan had finally come true. But according to her, being here had dredged up hurtful memories that I'd never dealt with.

Memories of Lochlan Powers, aka my archenemy.

See, Loch's mom and mine had been friends while in college, and when Mrs. Powers had opened a daycare, well, that's where I'd ended up when my mom decided to go back to work. So I'd practically known Loch since birth. We'd shared a crib a few times and had even once bathed together and Mom had the pictures to prove it. Ugh.

He and I had been buddies throughout elementary school, playing together on the playground and after school at his mom's daycare. But when we reached middle school things had changed. Since I didn't go to daycare anymore and the school we attended was bigger, we didn't see each other as often and kind of lost contact. Oh, I always kept an eye on him. How could I not when he was the cutest and coolest guy in school? He was naturally good at sports and made straight A's in class and all the girls adored him. Marcy had even once confessed to having had a slight crush on him.

But as for me? I'd been head over heels for him to an almost embarrassing degree. Yay me. Of course, he'd wanted nothing to do with the bespectacled, too-skinny, painfully shy, nerdy girl he'd grown up with who he often caught ogling him from afar. I hadn't been popular or a cheerleader or on the Student Council. No, I'd been timid and reticent and nothing but background noise to him.

Our sixth grade year, our moms had conspired (unbeknownst to me unfortunately) deciding it'd be a great idea for Loch to escort me to the Spring Dance. When he'd asked me, I'd almost fainted, having been so out-of-this-world excited at the prospect of getting to spend time with him again that I'd failed to see the annoyed look on his face.

And you've seen how that turned out.

So since my return to Seattle, the nightmares had come back with a vengeance and I'd had no idea until now that what had happened at the dance had apparently been so traumatic for me.

Wait. I take it back. That was me being a big fat liar.

I actually *did* know I'd been traumatized because I'd stayed upset for a very long time afterward. I mean, I'd been an impressionable twelve-year-old girl and Loch had definitely done a number on my already fragile ego.

I also knew that the way he'd behaved had ripped me to shreds and caused me to have all those crappy nightmares.

Moreover, I knew I'd crawled into a proverbial shell and shut everyone out my seventh through ninth grade years only making friends with Emmalynn Talbot who was the sweetest person ever and friends with everyone and was now at LSU majoring in petroleum engineering.

And I likewise knew that it had taken Coach Hawkins' coaxing me out of that shell at the end of my freshman year to get me to try out for the soccer team (which I'd made then played on the next three years and loved every minute of it).

Lastly, the biggest, most colossal thing I knew was that I hated Loch Powers.

A lot.

As in *a lot* a lot.

As in, if hate were planets, I'd be Jupiter, a lot.

I think you get the picture.

And, dang it, I was now pissed off to no end that I'd been such a frail little wilting flower of a girl who'd let a stupid boy's actions affect me to the extent that they had. But I wasn't going to let things get to me anymore because I was no longer the bashful, ugly, geeky girl he'd once insulted.

Well, crap. I take that back too. I'm still geeky but I can deal with that. Nothing wrong with being geeky.

Anyway, I wouldn't say I was beautiful, but instead of the pop-bottle-bottom glasses that had once graced my face, I now wore contacts that with their slight tint made my blue eyes appear bluer, and I also wore my auburn hair in long layers of loose curls most of the time instead of the two braids, ala Wednesday Addams, that I'd worn for years. Yeah, starting in fifth grade, I'd had an *Addams Family* thing going on. Tristan had had DVDs of both movies and I'd gone through a phase where I'd spent hours in my room watching them. Looking back, I think my infatuation with Wednesday was that she was so mean and said whatever she wanted and I think I wanted to be like that. But in ninth grade, I'd changed my look, having matured and finally grown out of my obsession with the awesome albeit macabre girl. After that I'd been hit on a few times by some very handsome guys so I didn't think I was lacking too much in the looks department. Also, soccer had been a great workout and made me proud of my fit body. I'd even once overheard a couple boys in my class saying something about my being built like a brick shithouse, which I think meant I had curves. I definitely had boobs and a booty and I dressed in a way that didn't overtly flaunt them but I didn't try hiding what I had either.

So that all being said, the relevancy of it was, I was stronger now, bolder, and if I happened to run into Loch, well, I told myself I'd no longer be intimidated by him. Nope, I'd stand up to him and would probably tell him what a jerk he'd been and how he'd almost ruined my life and that he could go take a hike.

Yep. That's exactly what I'd do.

Oh, and the very last thing I knew?

All my tough girl talk aside, I knew I was terrified to see him.

Confession Number Two

"I've only seen him a couple times over the past two years," Marcy was telling me as she spooned a bite of Honey Nut Cheerios into her mouth. Her dark hair was up in a messy bun and there was mascara smudged under her dark blue eyes. One of the straps of her tank top had fallen down to her tanned arm but she paid it no mind.

I put a bagel in the toaster. "Don't really care, Marce."

"Yeah, but I'm just preparing you in case you happen to run into him."

"There's what, over ten-thousand students on campus and you think I'm gonna run into him? And on the first day? Yeah, the odds are stacked pretty high." I rolled my eyes as I got the cream cheese out of the fridge.

We, of course, were talking about Loch. Goodie.

"I'm just saying that the Powers brothers have been a big deal at Hallervan for years, Sim. First of all, Zeke was voted Sexiest Man on Campus, like, every year. He was a big football star and is now playing in the pros. Gable was the hottest asshole you'd ever lay eyes on. He smiled at me once when I was walking across the quad and I think I blew an ovary. But he graduated last year and I'm pretty sure he's working for some architecture firm downtown. Ryker's now Mr. Intense and Studly Senior Wrestler, and I think every girl I've talked to wants to have his babies."

It was so weird hearing about these guys who I'd played with for years. Guys Loch and I had tormented constantly when we were little. I let out an exaggerated sigh as I turned to look at her. "And you're telling me all this because?"

She lifted the shoulder where the strap was hanging. "Getting you ready for your run-in with Loch."

I huffed out a barely there laugh as I spread cream cheese on my bagel. "Like I said, it's not likely that I'll run into him." I hoped.

She stood and carried her bowl to the sink. "Just warning you."

"Warning me about what?" I licked my thumb that had cream cheese on it then took my plate to the dining table and sat.

She turned and rested her butt against the sink crossing her arms over her chest and I saw she'd fixed her strap. "You remember Loch as a skinny sixth grader."

I took a bite. "Yeah? So?" I questioned, my voice garbled because of the food in my mouth. Classy, I know.

"He's hot now."

After taking a drink of orange juice, I looked at her. "He was hot then."

"Yeah, but he's *hot* now."

I shook my head and took another bite.

"Hot as in *man hot* not little boy hot," she went on to explain.

I was getting ticked off now because what did I care. "So he's hot. Big whoop. He's still an A-hole."

"Just don't say I didn't warn you." She pushed off the sink and made her way to the back door, plucking her keys off the holder we had on the wall. "All right, off to learn about drugs in Psychopharmacology class."

"Gonna be home for dinner?" I asked.

"It's Wednesday so Dr. Hoyt has late patients but he might cut me loose early."

"I'm making lasagna."

"Awesome. I'll tell him I already have to study for a test or something so I'll be home around five, 'kay? See ya later!" And she was out the door.

Marcy worked as a receptionist of sorts for a psychiatrist who was a family friend, which was good for her future career. I, on the other hand, worked at a secondhand gaming store which had no impact on my career but it was fun playing the games against the guys I worked with when business was slow, which was often.

After swallowing my last bite of bagel, I went to brush my teeth, giving myself a last going over in the mirror then headed to class.

~*~*~*~

I'd loved Hallervan's campus from the moment I'd first seen it.

When I was twelve, a few weeks before the fateful dance, I'd gone with Mom, who as a high school French teacher had taken her senior students on a spring tour of the language department. The whole place had felt exciting, all a-bustle with students hurrying to get to class, mingling in the Student Center, or hanging out on the quad studying, playing Frisbee or just tanning. On that same trip, Mom had told me about how when she and Dad had gone to Hallervan, she'd tutored him in French their sophomore year so he could keep his grades up, hence keeping his tennis scholarship, and how they'd ultimately fallen in love.

So today when I'd parked and gotten out of my Jeep, it had felt right, like coming home.

"Mom! I know you're teaching, but I had to leave a message. I just walked by the tennis court where Dad played. This is so cool! Anyway, I'll call you tonight to let you know how it went. Love you! Bye!"

	Walking to my Intro to Algorithms class (I was definitely a geek) I was excited to continue with my degree of becoming a software engineer here at Hallervan. When I got to the amphitheater where my class was held, I saw it was packed (guess there were lots of other computer geeks here too) and walking up the middle aisle through several other students, I made it to the fourth of the five rows of curved tables and found an empty seat next to a really cute guy who I smiled at shyly. He smiled back then kind of made a show of reaching to his right to hold the hand of the pretty girl next to him. Well, all right then.

	I rolled my eyes as I got out my notebook then thought about my boyfriend Jared who I'd left behind at Berkeley. Well, I guess I should say ex-boyfriend now. He and I had dated for almost a year but for some reason I just hadn't been feeling it. I mean, he was nice and all, attractive with a great body, but it had always seemed like something was missing. So when I decided I'd be attending Hallervan, we'd talked about how it didn't make sense for us to stay together and we'd had a fairly amicable breakup (I think he'd felt the same about us which was why he didn't get too upset) but we promised to keep in contact. Matter of fact, he'd texted me this morning to wish me luck on my first day. His classes didn't start until tomorrow, so I'd wished him the same. He'd also reminded me that he had some friends here so if he made it up to see them, he'd call so we could get together and have lunch or something which had made me happy that we could be so chill with each other.

	As I smiled at this, Dr. Lykins, the professor, came in, took a look around the full room then jumped right into his lecture about asymptotic analysis and Big-O notation. Of course, there were the usual snickers at the mention of "Big-O" and Dr. Lykins even chuckled a bit saying he knew that was coming and his pun made everyone laugh even more. Then he got right to it and before I knew it, I had an entire page filled with notes.

	I flipped my notebook page over ready to scribble more and had the weirdest feeling that someone was watching me, so bringing my head up I glanced around the room for a moment, looking first to my right through the sea of faces busy listening to the lecture or furiously scrawling on their paper as I'd been, then to my left and was instantly met with the most gorgeous pair of chestnut eyes surrounded by long, sable lashes gazing back at me which almost made me drop my pencil.

Holy smokes!

And the guy the eyes belonged to was hot! His dark caramel hair was short on the sides but longer on top which he'd combed back and I could tell he hadn't used any gel or pomade in it because it lay softly in an array of fashionable messiness. He had a perfect, straight nose and his hollow cheeks and chiseled jaw made me think he might be a model. Dang! I stared back watching completely mesmerized as his mouth slowly tipped up into a smile. It was only then that I realized I was gawking at him, and I became flustered, my eyes going huge as I whipped my head around to face the front. I then let out a little gasp of surprise as my pencil flipped out of my hand and over in front of Cute Guy next to me. I could sense his frown as he turned toward me and handed it back. Glancing sheepishly at him as I took it, I pushed some hair behind my ear in embarrassment which made him squint his eyes at me in disapproval then turn away.

For the rest of the class, I did that thing all women do, you know, where you act like something's *so* much more interesting other than what you really want to be looking at, which in my case was to see whether Mr. Hottie McTottie, who may very well have been the most handsome man I'd ever laid eyes on, was still gazing at me. Instead, I found myself taking notes with such forced concentration it was almost as if the state of the free world rested on whether I crossed my "T's" just so. Lame.

When class was over and Dr. Lykins had told us class wouldn't meet Friday, I made a note of it then gathered my things and as I stood to go I had to wring my hand a bit to get the cramp out of it from gripping my pencil so hard. Then turning to leave, I ran smack dab into a wall of white t-shirt covered by a faded blue denim button up with the sleeves rolled up to the elbows.

"Sorry!" I exclaimed then my eyes went big when they landed on the tee that clung to well-defined pecs. Nice! I next noticed the muscular forearms that were attached to hands that were resting on my waist. Whoa! My eyes shot up to see who was being so bold as to put their hands on me that way (even though he'd probably done it to stop me from running into him) and also to see who this amazing body belonged to and I swear, if I'd still had that stupid pencil in my hand, it probably would've flown up to stick in the ceiling when I realized it was Smiling Model Guy who was all up in my space. Gah!

"Hey," he said as one side of his mouth curled up into a half grin while his umber eyes glittered mischievously at me as if he knew exactly the effect he was having on me.

Just being this close to him was making me have to focus on getting my breathing under control before I passed out. Man, I seriously needed to work on my hot guy interaction skills.

When an "H" sound puffed out of my mouth before I finally got my wits about me enough to utter the complete word, "Hi," I wanted to smack myself.

Then things just kept getting better because I continued standing there like a total fool, enthralled with the fact that his eyes had flecks of gold in them. But when I saw the sides of them crinkle I realized he was laughing at me. Shaking myself out of the hypnotic hot-guy-all-up-in-my-face state I was in, I took a hasty step back making his hand drop from my waist. Then I really felt dumb because I saw the reason why he'd been chuckling at me. He'd been holding his other hand out for me to shake the whole time. Oh. Mentally chastising myself for being such a dimwit, I internally rolled my eyes as I now held out my own hand to his.

His huge hand enveloped mine then he squeezed gently. "Hey," he repeated, his eyes dancing with humor at having to start over again.

I couldn't help but huff out a laugh at how ridiculously I'd behaved. "Hi."

"You new here?"

He kept holding my hand but instead of being uncomfortable, I found that I really quite liked it and kind of hoped he continued doing it.

"Um, yeah. Well, I was actually born here but my family moved away when I was little." I lifted a shoulder. "But now I'm back."

"Well, welcome back." He grinned now and my eyes landed on his perfect mouth. Wow. "I'd be glad to show you around sometime if you'd like."

My eyes darted up to his because, gosh, how nice was he? As his deep, soulful eyes held mine prisoner the shiver that ran through me confused me because I'd never reacted this way to a guy before.

But as our eyes remained locked, something weird happened. Mine now narrowed and I canted my head to the side as I took him in because it suddenly seemed that there was something so familiar about him, I just couldn't put my finger on it. Still, come on, no way would I forget someone who looked as good as he did. That amazing hair, those perfect lips, the flawless face, the cocky attitude.

And then it came to me and it felt like a giant fist plowed into my gut.

No!

No, no, no!

My mortal enemy was standing right in front of me and he was holding my hand!

Oh, my God. Could the odds that were so stacked in my favor have really come crashing down this quickly?

My eyes remained squinted as they quickly roamed over his face and I watched as his narrowed a bit too as if he recognized me also. I watched engrossed as he frowned and blinked, then he dropped my hand and pulled his head back as if to say, "Could it really be Simone?" I was even more rapt when I caught the emotions crossing his face that looked like, "No! It couldn't be *her*! No way could she have turned out to look somewhat decent!" And that's when I became a tad angry then just flat-out pissed when the look disappeared altogether and I knew he'd convinced himself that there was no way it could be me.

Jerk.

"Uh, sure. That would be nice," I responded weakly, hating that being near him was turning me back into the insecure little wimp I'd once been.

"It's a date then," he answered with a wink.

And even though I was convinced it was him, I had to know for sure, so I casually inquired, "So, how long have you gone to Hallervan?" and was surprised at how nonchalant it came out.

"This is my third year. My family's from Seattle. Matter of fact, I've had two brothers graduate from here already. My other brother's a senior this year and we're the last two, so I guess we're kind of a keystone here." He chuckled.

I bit my lips and nodded slowly. It was definitely him. Marcy was going to flip when she heard this.

"Can I see your phone?" he requested making me frown for a second. Consequently, my mind hovered between giving it to him or telling him where he could stick it, but not wanting to cause a scene, I complied, digging it out of my bag and handing it to him. As I watched his thumbs move over the screen, I couldn't help but think how surreal this was, how strange and completely bizarre.

Loch Powers was standing here nine years after he'd humiliated me and he had no idea who I was.

When his phone rang, he pulled it out of his pocket and handed mine back. "Now I've got your number and you've got mine." And, lord, that smile of his was so dazzling it made me want to sigh. My brow came down as I reminded myself I was not going to be sucked into his sexy wiles. Ever.

His phone now chimed and I saw his brow come down too as he read a text message. "Fuck. I've gotta go." He looked up at me and gave me his grin again. "How about you text me so we can make arrangements, okay?" I nodded then drew in a sharp breath when he ran the backs of his knuckles down my cheek, his eyes warm on mine. "Later," he mumbled giving me another wink then he left.

I walked out of class stunned. How in the world had that just happened? As I strode to my next class, all I could do was shake my head at the events that had just transpired. Then my phone buzzed that I'd received a text. I blinked a couple times as I glanced at it because things had just gotten real.

Text Message—Wed, Aug. 13, 11:17 a.m.

Loch Powers: Hey again. Guess I was so blown away by your beauty I forgot to get your name. I'm Loch, by the way. Very nice meeting you. Hope to hear from you soon, gorgeous…

Frippity fracking frap! This was just all kinds of crazy. I glared at my phone for a couple more seconds then stomped the rest of the way to my next class probably looking like a goof as I did but whatever. Once inside the classroom and being seated, I pulled my notebook and pencil out of my bag then threw my phone inside it not wanting to look at it again. Oh, he'd be hearing from me soon, all right.

And, boy, was I going to give him an earful.

Confession Number Three

"This is perfect!" Marcy said after I accosted her the minute she walked in the door that night and told her what had happened at class.

"How? How is this perfect?" I countered, freaking out a bit at her lackadaisical attitude.

"Let me change first and we'll talk. Is the lasagna ready yet?" she asked as she walked toward her room.

"Five more minutes for the bread. Hurry!" I heard her chuckle. Ugh. I wanted to talk now but whatever. I could give her time to change. I guessed. In the kitchen I put the bread in the oven and paced a bit wondering how my running into my biggest adversary was perfect. I'd just gotten the bread out and was brushing it with butter when she finally came in.

"Smells great!" she announced as she pulled a bottle of wine from the fridge. "Yeah?" she asked and I nodded. While she poured the wine and set our glasses on the table she told me about her classes that morning then we both prepared our plates and sat. "What's this salad dressing?" she inquired as she chewed, stabbing to get another forkful of lettuce.

"Tristan and Sky brought it back from Italy last month. She called earlier so I ran over and got it. It's good, isn't it?" My brother and his girlfriend Skylar, yes, the same girlfriend he'd had in high school, now lived together in a gorgeous house in a pretty swanky part of Seattle. He and I were both following in Dad's footsteps by going the computer route which thrilled Dad to no end. Tris was a software engineer (which was what I was wanting to do) for a large company and making bank, well on his way to becoming a manager, and Sky worked at an interior design firm and was quickly building a clientele with her amazing skills. With the salaries they were pulling in, they were doing quite well and since they both loved traveling, they were taking advantage of it.

"It's awesome," Marcy garbled, mouth full.

"Nice, Marce." I took a drink, felt I'd waited the necessary amount of time to keep from appearing crazed to hear what she had to say, then attacked the elephant in the room. "Okay, so how is it perfect that I ran into Loch?"

She grinned, her azure eyes dancing with mischief. "Wondered how long you'd hold out." She smiled at my eyebrow raise. "Okay, running into him isn't the perfect part. The perfect part is you're gonna go out with him." When I started to protest she held up her hand. "Let me finish."

"Doesn't sound so perfect to me..." I muttered.

"It will, though!"

"You're way too excited. Does this involve some kind of psychological experiment or something?"

She laughed. "Hm. Hadn't thought of that. I could use it as my thesis for Dr. Stone's class. *The Enigmatic Psychology of Revenge* by Marcy Belton. I like the sound of that."

"Quit stalling. What do you have up your sleeve, Marce?"

"All right, here's what you're gonna do, you'll go out with him. And you'll have a good time."

"But—"

"You'll wow him with your gorgeous self and your dry sense of humor."

"But—"

"I'm sure he'll ask your name, so you'll tell him it's Celeste, you know, your middle name—"

"Yeah, I know my middle name. But—"

"Just don't add St. John because he might make the connection."

"But—"

"Then when the evening's over and you've dazzled him, totally made him enamored with you, he'll bring you home, probably make a move for a goodnight kiss then BOOM! You tell him who you really are. Tell him what an asshole jerk he was and probably still is, then come inside and slam the door in his face."

I sat and stared at her because that was a very evil plan. And I hate to say it, but a part of me, a kind of very big part of me, liked it.

"Or, you can do it in front of people like he did to you. That would even be better." She raised her eyebrows as she added this last part letting me know public humiliation was her preference.

"Um, you do realize you're twenty-one and I'll be twenty-one in a month?"

"So?" She looked genuinely confused.

I snorted. "Well, this is something a middle school kid would do, isn't it? It's also pretty mean, don't you think?"

"No."

We sat staring at each other as I flipped her little scheme over and over in my mind and wondered why she was so gung-ho on getting him back.

"Look, he was a dick—" she began.

"We were sixth graders!" I answered, still not getting her. I mean, I had a reason to hate him. And I appreciated that she was looking out for me but I didn't get her enthusiasm over it.

"When you were in sixth grade didn't you know that what he did was wrong? C'mon, Simone. He should've known better but he went ahead and hurt you really bad anyway. He deserves to finally be put in his place."

"I've got three classes with him! If I do this, I'll have to see him every Monday, Wednesday and Friday!"

"Even better!" Marcy exclaimed practically jumping up and down in her chair as she did baby claps.

"I don't know..." And I didn't. First of all, I didn't like being deceptive. Second, if I went through with it, I'd have to spend an entire evening with him and that didn't sound like a good plan at all. Third, did I really want revenge so much that I'd knowingly hurt him? And fourth... "What's in it for you?"

"I have my reasons," she shared cryptically with a frown then took a drink. "Plus, if you do this, it'll probably stop the nightmares. You know you hate the nightmares," she goaded.

"Yeah." I nodded then let out a sigh. "So how am I supposed to pull this off?"

"Call him. Text him. Doesn't matter. I know! Invite him to the Kappa Sigs' back-to-school party this Friday night. It's a pool party so we need to dig our bikinis out for a last hurrah! Adam's supposed to pick me up at eight, so you need to have Loch get you after so he doesn't see me. The couple times I've seen him around, he knew who I was because, well, we graduated high school together. So what do you think?"

I shrugged grudgingly.

"Look, I know you're a nice girl, Sim. I get it. But this dillweed needs to pay for what he did to… to you. I mean, I remember talking to you the first couple years after you moved and you didn't even sound like yourself. That wasn't right. And it's all on him." She took a bite of bread. "I don't think it's right that he got away with what he did. I'm your best friend and I just wanna see your nightmares stop, okay?"

"And humiliating him will do that?"

"Well, yeah."

I still wasn't buying it wholly and she knew this.

"Okay, does it help if I tell you about what he did to Samantha Hays our freshman year? You remember her. She was such a sweetheart. Not really popular but always so nice to everyone. Well, I'm pretty sure Loch's friends teased him about her having a crush on him. And I guess he couldn't stand to have someone who wasn't a cheerleader or whatever liking him. You wanna know what he did?"

Did I want to know? Yeesh. I gave her a cautious nod.

"We were in line in the cafeteria. Samantha's dad had just been laid off so she was embarrassed that she'd had to get on the free lunch plan. So Loch walks up to her and snatches her lunch card out of her hand, looks at it then holds it up while announcing to the entire school that she's getting her lunch for free."

I scoffed. "He did not!" At her "Oh, yes he did" look, I sputtered, "W-what? That's horrible!" I remembered Samantha and how adorable she'd been and knew that must've really hurt her.

"Yep. She ended up transferring to Jefferson at the semester because everyone teased her so much about it." Marcy nodded at my horrified look then she remembered something else. "Oh! He and Mary Fletcher dated for like two weeks our sophomore year when she asked if he'd help at the homeless shelter the day before Thanksgiving. She said he'd been all enthusiastic about it but when he didn't show up, she called him to ask where he was and he acted like he had no idea what she was talking about and she could hear a girl giggling in the background. When Mary told him she still had his text messages telling her he'd be there, he told her he didn't have time for her, that he'd moved on and that she needed to 'get over him.'"

"Wow," I mumbled.

"As far as I know, he's still just as cocky and as big of a jerk now as he was then. So do these other girls' stories change your mind?"

I blew out a breath as I picked at my lasagna with my fork still not convinced I wanted to do it.

"All right. I didn't want to tell you, but Loch also did something that embarrassed the shit outta me too."

My head snapped up at this. Ah, here it came, the real reason she wanted him shot down. "What? What'd he do to you?"

Her face turned bright red and I knew it had to be bad because it took a lot for Marcy to get embarrassed. "It's so mortifying, Sim." She took a breath and blew it out. "So the beginning of seventh grade, we were in science class getting ready to dissect frogs. Jenna Plum and I were partners and Loch and David Janzen were partners and at the same table Jenna and I were. You remember what a huge crush I had on David, right?"

I nodded wondering what the heck Loch had done to her that made her still so uncomfortable to this day.

"I was a little squeamish because, well, frogs," she shuddered, "so pretty much the whole time, Jenna was having to do the cutting and I was leaning on the table trying not to pass out. Halfway through class, Loch starts looking at me funny and I'm frowning wondering what the hell's wrong with him. Then he suddenly lunges toward me and grabs… this is so humiliating…" She put her head in her hand and let out a groan.

"What? What did he do?"

She slowly raised her head and grimaced. "He pulled a tissue out of my shirt."

I wasn't making the connection and frowned trying to figure out what exactly she was saying.

"I stuffed my bra, Simone! I mean, all the girls had sprouted boobs except for me and it was embarrassing. So I started stuffing every day to make myself feel better. I guess when I was leaning over, it pushed a tissue out."

I had to bite my lips to keep from laughing because that was cute that she'd done that but when I saw that she had tears in her eyes, I felt horrible. Reaching a hand out to cover hers, I said, "Oh, honey, I'm sorry. I'm so sorry I wasn't there to stand up for you like you did for me. Why didn't you tell me about this?"

She swiped a tear away and let out a humorless laugh as I sat back. "I didn't want to add to your misery. You already hated him and always sounded so sad whenever we talked, I just thought it'd be best to stay quiet. And I know it's stupid for me to still be upset about it, but it was so degrading especially with David being right there! The worst part was after he pulled the tissue out he started twirling it around asking me what it was and everyone started laughing. Everybody called me Stuffy the rest of the year." She snorted. "It's silly now, but it definitely wasn't at the time." She tried hiding it but I could see the hurt in her face. And then she shrugged. "So now you know why I hate him too and want him to pay for all the shit he did to people."

He *was* a jerk! And because she was my best friend and I felt like I'd failed her for not being there to have her back, I agreed. "Okay, I'll do it. But not just for me, for you too. And for Samantha and Mary. You're right. He needs to know what a... what an asshole he was."

"Why, Simone St. John! Your momma's gonna come up here and wash your mouth out with soap!" she replied with a giggle.

I usually tried not to curse unless I was really mad or the circumstances deemed it necessary. It was something that my parents had pounded into Tristan's and my head (it didn't take so much with him) but right now, I felt this situation warranted some foul language.

I scowled at my best friend. "Well, I'm bigger than my mom now, so I'd like to see her try."

This made Marcy snort. "You're really gonna do it? I mean, honestly, I know I should let it go but he was such a prick."

"Yeah, I am. He needs to go down."

She reached her palm up and I gave her a high five. "Awesome. You fuckin' rock, Sim."

~*~*~*~

Text Message—Weds, Aug. 13, 10:38 p.m.

Me: Hey, so there's a Kappa Sig party Friday. Wanna go?

I was lying in bed having commenced Campaign Conquer the Cocksucker, or Triple C (Marcy's chosen title of our operation) and waiting for an answer.

Text Message—Weds, Aug. 13, 11:02 p.m.

Assface (Marcy had decided this was a more appropriate name for him in my phone)**: Hey! Sounds good. I didn't get your name today...**

Text Message—Weds, Aug. 13, 11:04 p.m.

Me: Celeste

Text Message—Weds, Aug. 13, 11:05 p.m.

Assface: I like it. It's very pretty... like you

What a flirt. I hated that I couldn't take anything he said to heart though because all he'd been since we'd "met" today was very sweet and I really wished I could believe him.

Text Message—Weds, Aug. 13, 11:05 p.m.

Me: Thank you.

Text Message—Weds, Aug. 13, 11:05 p.m.

Assface: So does this mean I'll get to see you in a bikini?

Text Message—Weds, Aug. 13, 11:05 p.m.

Me: Well, it is a pool party... does this mean I get to see YOU in a bikini?

Text Message—Weds, Aug. 13, 11:06 p.m.

Assface: First of all, can't wait to see your gorgeous body in it. Second, how about a mankini? I've got a bright yellow one. Would that work?

I snorted out a laugh at that visual.

Text Message—Weds, Aug. 13, 11:06 p.m.

Me: Absolutely. Can't wait to see your gorgeous body in it

Text Message—Weds, Aug. 13, 11:06 p.m.

Assface: You like my body, huh?

Well, crap. He had some serious flirting skills. I was still stuck in Flirting 101 and knew I needed to be careful here.

Text Message—Weds, Aug. 13, 11:07 p.m.

Me: It'll do

Text Message—Weds, Aug. 13, 11:07 p.m.

Assface: It'll do...

Text Message—Weds, Aug. 13, 11:07 p.m.

Me: Yeah, it'll do

Text Message—Weds, Aug. 13, 11:07 p.m.

Assface: Baby, I'll show you what it can do one of these days

Yikes! *Be super cold, Simone.*

Text Message—Weds, Aug. 13, 11:08 p.m.

Me: Think so, huh?

Text Message—Weds, Aug. 13, 11:08 p.m.

Assface: Know so

Text Message—Weds, Aug. 13, 11:08 p.m.

Me: Well, you're not arrogant at all

Text Message—Weds, Aug. 13, 11:08 p.m.

Assface: Hm. Arrogant? I like to think of myself as having seemly swagger or maybe even inspired insolence

Text Message—Weds, Aug. 13, 11:09 p.m.

Me: Someone knows their alliteration

Text Message—Weds, Aug. 13, 11:09 p.m.

Assface: I'm nothing if not well educated. So... back to this bikini of yours...

Text Message—Weds, Aug. 13, 11:09 p.m.

Me: What about it?

Text Message—Weds, Aug. 13, 11:09 p.m.

Assface: Color?

Text Message—Weds, Aug. 13, 11:09 p.m.

Me: Why do you need to know the color?

Text Message—Weds, Aug. 13, 11:10 p.m.

Assface: So I know what color cummerbund to wear to match

I snorted out another laugh. Dang it. I was trying so hard to be indifferent, which I knew was coming off as just plain rude, but this was tricky!

Text Message—Weds, Aug. 13, 11:10 p.m.

Me: If you must know, it's royal blue

Text Message—Weds, Aug. 13, 11:10 p.m.

Assface: Hot. I'll bet you look amazing in it

Text Message—Weds, Aug. 13, 11:10 p.m.

Me: Look, I know you're just trying to be nice, so you can save the flattery

Text Message—Weds, Aug. 13, 11:11 p.m.

Assface: Truth isn't flattery, darlin'

"Shit!" I muttered then realized I'd cursed. "Damn it!"

Text Message—Weds, Aug. 13, 11:11 p.m.

Me: And you're quite charming too, aren't you?

Text Message—Weds, Aug. 13, 11:11 p.m.

Assface: I try to be. Is it working?

Text Message—Weds, Aug. 13, 11:12 p.m.

Me: How many girls have you charmed out of their bikini bottoms, Loch?

Text Message—Weds, Aug. 13, 11:12 p.m.

Assface: There's only one I can think of right now I'd like to do it to

All right. This had to end now because he was getting to me!

Text Message—Weds, Aug. 13, 11:12 p.m.

Me: I have an early class, so I need to go

Text Message—Weds, Aug. 13, 11:12 p.m.

Assface: Okay. If I don't get to talk to you in class Friday, I'll pick you up at 8?

No! That was when Marcy said Adam was picking her up.

Text Message—Weds, Aug. 13, 11:12 p.m.

Me: How about 8:30?

Text Message—Weds, Aug. 13, 11:12 p.m.

Assface: Can do. Sweet dreams, beautiful...

How nice was he?

Well, this was going to be fun seeing if I could withstand his flirting. Just what had I gotten myself into?

Confession Number Four

I was panicking, throwing clothes all over my room as I dug through my dresser drawers. I had on my bikini and wedge sandals and must've looked like a Pamela Anderson wannabe which only added to my torment. Ugh.

"Jesus. What's happening in here?" Marcy asked from my doorway.

"I can't find my cover-up! I know it's here!" I flung out some t-shirts and shorts looking for the stupid thing.

"I borrowed it Monday, remember?"

I stood up straight and looked at my roommate then it dawned on me. "Oh, yeah." Glancing around my room which looked like a tornado had just passed through I huffed out a breath.

"Stop being so nervous, Sim. It's gonna be okay. Really."

I put my hands on my hips and raised my eyebrows at her. "You're not at this very moment having to prepare yourself to be the poster girl for all things revenge, now are you? If you were in my shoes, you'd be feeling the same way," I challenged.

She slowly nodded in agreement. "You're right. Okay, carry on being nervous then." When I shot her a look, she snorted. "I'll go get your cover-up."

It was almost eight which meant Loch would be here in thirty minutes and I could feel myself starting to come apart beneath the surface. As I waited for Marcy to return, I figured standing and waiting was futile, so I started nabbing clothes off the floor and shoving them back into my drawers which helped a bit with the nerves.

"Here it is. This thing is so sexy, Sim! Loch's gonna be drooling like crazy then BAM! you're gonna shut him down like that!" She snapped her fingers then threw me the white crocheted cover-up that I was now second guessing wearing.

"Maybe we should trade," I suggested.

"Hell no. This thing's basically a muumuu and coming off the minute I get there," she retorted about the semi-ugly housedress looking thing she was wearing.

"Then what about the UDub tee Tristan gave me?"

Marcy tilted her head to the side and looked at me in disgust. "That thing swallows you."

"Exactly."

"No! You wanna look hot and make him want you! That's part of the plan!"

I held the cover-up out in front of me. "But this thing leaves nothing to the imagination."

"I know. Adam loved it on me." She giggled which made me roll my eyes. And speaking of Adam, just then he texted her the same time he rang the doorbell. "He's here! I'll see you there, okay?" At what I'm sure was a terrified look on my face, she said, "It's gonna be fine, Sim. I'll be there so if you start feeling uncomfortable, text me and Adam and I will come find you. And look, if Triple C doesn't work, it's no big deal. Go have fun and if it works, it works, okay? If it doesn't, we'll put Triple C Part Deux into action."

"I can only imagine what that entails. G-strings and pasties?"

"Maybe…" She chuckled at my opened-mouth look of shock. "Just kidding. But it'll be fine. 'Kay! I'll either see you there or talk to you tonight! If not, wish me luck! Bye!" She rushed out of the room.

She and Adam had started dating this past Sunday, so not even a week, and I'd met him Monday. He seemed like a pretty nice guy and he was really into Marcy which was good. She'd been giddy and excited all week telling me she thought tonight would be the first time they had sex which was why she wanted me to wish her luck.

"Okay, yeah, bye. Good luck to you and your vagina," I muttered then had to chuckle a moment later when I heard her squeal after she opened the front door telling Adam he looked hot.

When I heard the front door close, I sighed then pulled on the cover-up and checked myself out in my full-length mirror. Boy, it was absolutely sexy in its barely-there coverage and clinginess and I tugged at the hem trying to make it longer which just made it spring back up to its original indecent length. I'd actually bought it thinking Jared would like it (he definitely had) but this was different. I mean, it was one thing to wear it for my then boyfriend, but to wear it now seemed kind of risqué to me. I vacillated for a few minutes on whether I should wear a pair of shorts under it and that's when the doorbell rang again.

Crap! He was early!

Taking a deep breath and blowing it out I looked at my reflection. "You hate Loch Powers. He was a jerk to you and others. Make him pay," I reminded myself. I nodded, blowing out another breath, then went to get the door, snagging my keys off the hook and slipping them into the one pocket my cover-up had then grabbed the towels I'd gotten for us.

"Hey," I said when I opened the door, looking up at the freaking gorgeous god who was standing on my front porch.

His eyes roved over my body (twice!) before his eyes met mine and, oh my, it didn't take a genius to read what was in those eyes of his.

Flat-out lust burned from them which made me let out a little gasp. "Hey, beautiful."

My face flamed red hot and I had to tell myself to stay calm. Easier said than done. Jeez. "Hey. Uh, you ready?"

"As I'll ever be," he answered with a grin taking the towels from me and tucking them under his arm then he grabbed my hand and pulled me out the door as I tugged it closed behind me with my other hand. Then he executed some kind of yank on the hand he was holding and I ended up flush against his body where my palms landed against his rock hard chest. Holy cow. He wrapped his arm around me, his hand resting just above my butt, his fingers clamping onto the crocheted material of my cover-up and pulled me against him. "I take it back. I've been ready since Wednesday." His head dipped closer to mine as he said this until his lips were now against mine and I felt them move when he said, "Dreamed how you'd look and it doesn't fucking come close. You're stunning, Celeste." Then he kissed me. And, man-oh-man, could he kiss. It started slow with just his mouth on mine, which was very nice, but when I felt his tongue gliding across my bottom lip I pulled in a startled breath and that's when his tongue entered my mouth and, well, now we were full-on making out.

Even as my brain was screaming at me to stop, one of my hands made its way up to the side of his waist as the other wound its way behind his neck where my fingers clutched his hair as our tongues twisted together exquisitely making me moan into his mouth. My moan seemed to trigger his arms into moving fast, I felt the towels drop and the next thing I knew, one arm had cinched its way around my waist holding me even more tightly to him as the other made its way up to where his hand held the side of my face. Then he buried his fingers in the hair behind my ear clutching it to keep my mouth firmly against his. Wow.

I don't know how long the kiss lasted, a couple minutes, I do know that much, but it wasn't until I suddenly realized that in accordance with the motion of our kiss and the way our tongues were jousting with each other, it became clear to me that I was rocking my body into his, as in mock humping him(!), practically having clothed (kind of) vertical sex with him as my hand at his waist dug in to pull him with me in my libidinous thrusts against him and I froze. My eyes flew open wide and locked with his that had also opened when I went all statue on him but our mouths remained connected.

Then I felt him grin against my lips and I pushed him away.

"I-I'm so sorry," I stammered, my eyes looking anywhere but at him, shocked that I'd practically molested him right there on my front porch.

He grabbed my hand and bent to get me to look in his eyes. "Baby, you have nothing to be sorry for except the fact that we stopped." He smirked.

I closed my eyes for a second, once again angry that I'd let him get the best of me. I had a plan to follow, darn it! It took me a moment, but when I opened my eyes, it was settled. That would not be happening again. *I* was going to be in charge from now on come hell or high water; I just needed to display a little confidence, whether it be feigned or real, to keep him off balance. And the displaying of the confidence had to start now. So with a little "humph" and a flip of my hair behind my shoulder I turned and walked to the blue pickup truck that was in the driveway, putting a little extra swing in my hips to tease him, maybe addle his brain a bit, which I didn't know if it worked or not but it was worth a shot. When I was almost to the truck, I looked over my shoulder at him and said flippantly, "You coming?" As I continued walking, I thought I was being so cool until I heard him mumble from behind me, "Not yet, gorgeous," which made me stumble on my heels. Darn it.

I reached for the handle of the pickup but he was there faster, opening it and helping me inside then closing the door. I kept my eyes on him as he walked around the front, all Tony Stark cool himself, and I envied the fact that he just exuded an amazing amount of aplomb while I had to work at it. But I could do it. I mean, I was smart. I should be able to master sangfroid even if I had to fake my way through, right?

And watching him, I knew I was positively going to have to fake it because he looked freaking hot in the white Hallervan tank top he wore over his navy board shorts. He also had a little scruff that just enhanced his already beautiful face. Lord.

"Buckle up, buttercup," he remarked when he got in the truck giving me a wink. I did as he said as he turned the key in the ignition then backed out of the drive, asking, "That your Jeep?" when we passed it.

"Yes."

"Nice," he replied with a nod, now putting the truck in gear and heading to the frat house. "I thought of getting a Jeep but got Roadie instead." He rubbed the dash of his truck then patted it like it was his dog or something.

"Roadie?" I asked.

He turned his head toward me and grinned then he looked back at the road. "You know, *Road House*?"

I stared at him and blinked.

At my silence, he gave me a quick glance. "*Road House*? Swayze? Elliot?" He gave me another look and I shook my head and you'd have thought I'd broken a major law or something at the expression on his face. "You know, 'Pain don't hurt'?" He glanced at the road before turning my way again. When I blinked again still not sure what he was talking about, his head turned toward the front but he continued. "'I'll get all the sleep I need when I'm dead'? How about, 'I thought you'd be bigger'?"

I couldn't help the giggle that escaped seeing how frustrated he'd become and I bit my lips to keep from full-on laughing.

"Babe." The look of disappointment on his face made me snort now. "Seriously? You've never seen *Road House*?" When I shook my head again, he gave me a side eye then shook his too. "Gotta remedy that. That movie's like a piece of Americana!" He reached over and took my hand, sliding his fingers through mine then rested the back of his on the console.

"Is it a, uh, guy movie?" I ventured.

He now regarded me with utter disbelief and I finally did laugh. "It's a movie for *everyone*. Nothing short of iconic." He shook his head again as he watched the road but I saw his lips twitch so I knew he was mostly teasing.

"Guess I'll have to check it out."

"Damn straight," he muttered as he gave my hand a squeeze then started smoothing his thumb slowly over the top of mine.

Oh my.

Amidst my shivering at just his touch, I suddenly sobered at the thought that I was in Loch Powers' truck wearing a bikini and going to a party after having just made out with him. After having watched him treat his vehicle like it was a canine (which was ridiculous) then seeing him almost getting upset because I didn't know what movie he was talking about. Loch Powers who I hated, no, *loathed*, who at the end of the night I was going to call out for being a jerk for the way he'd treated me and I felt my stomach drop.

I was such a witch.

To take my mind off this, I inquired, "So what're you majoring in?" I knew it was something computer-related, of course, but didn't know the specifics.

"Not sure. Maybe an IT Manager or security engineer. Or software engineer. Hell, any of them will do. What about you?"

"Software engineer. My brother, Tris—" Crap. Would he remember Tristan's name? Crap! "Uh, my brother's an engineer here in Seattle and he loves it, so that's influenced me a lot."

He nodded just as we pulled onto the street where the party was. "Fuck me," he muttered because there were people and cars everywhere. "Gonna have to park a couple blocks away, I think."

He drove on and I was shocked at how many people there were. Jared and I had gone to a couple parties at Berkeley and it never ceased to amaze me how many students showed up for them, but for some reason, I thought since Hallervan was smaller there'd be fewer people. Color me all kinds of wrong.

The most shocking thing of all, though, was that there was an enormous fiberglass waterslide a ways off. I'd seen people working on something when I'd left class earlier but hadn't realized that's what it was. Yikes.

A block down the street, Loch pulled into the drive of a small house and parked. At my questioning look, he replied, "My buddy Nick's place. I'll owe him." He winked at me and I felt my heart seize. God!

When he got out of the truck, coming around to help me out of my side and taking my hand leading me toward the festivities, the guilt I felt was almost crippling because he was being so nice. Man, who was the jerk now?

"What *is* this place?" I asked as we walked toward a huge sports complex and a football field with all its lights on.

"It's where extracurricular sports are played. Some rich dude from Seattle donated millions for it. Guess he didn't make the varsity football team when he went here and now he's a multimillionaire so building all this was a big fuck you to the coach who didn't let him play." He shrugged. "What's up, Walk?" he asked a guy who was giving a girl a piggyback ride as they went by us.

The guy turned around with a grin and said, "Not much, man. Ready to get this party started, though!" Then he took off in a gallop making the girl on his back scream with laughter.

"Hey, Loch," several girls in a group called as we went by, the greeting turning into four syllables instead of two with their flirty tone.

"How's it going, ladies?" he answered giving them a grin.

"It's going great, handsome!" one seriously pretty girl answered. "Don't forget to call me and let me know when you're picking me up tomorrow night!"

Ergh.

Loch held his hand up but didn't look back at her as he said, "Sure, Alyssa, whatever." Then I heard him snort and he squeezed my hand in his. "Ignore her. She and my brother Gable hooked up for like, five minutes. She's a bitch who likes to stir shit up."

As we walked, I bit my lip and looked down at my strappy sandals wondering why I even cared. "Have *you* hooked up with her?"

This got me a chuckle. "Fuck no. Not to be a prick, but I think I'm pretty smart and able to make decent decisions. Gable, on the other hand, when he was here? Liked pussy. A lot. Wasn't too picky either."

"You sure do cuss a lot," I blurted. Whoops. Giving him a quick glance with my shocked face I looked away with a cringe at the fact that my observation had been vocalized. I mean, his cussing didn't really bother me because Tristan talked exactly the same way so that had just slipped out.

Now he barked out a laugh, stopped walking, put his hands on my shoulders and turned me to face him then leaned down so we were eye-to-eye. "Babe."

My eyes went back and forth on his as I saw the golden flecks practically sparkling in them. When he said nothing more, I whispered, "What?"

"You grew up with my brothers, you'd cuss a lot too. I'll try to tone it down but can't promise anything." He smiled then leaned in and brushed his lips against mine and then we were walking again, my hand in his.

Did I say the guilt was now about to eat me alive?

We kept walking getting closer to the field and I started seeing beer kegs everywhere with students mulling around filling their cups to the brim. There were even impromptu ping pong tables around made out of sheets of plywood and sawhorses where kids were playing beer pong. Also? There were assorted swimming pools *everywhere* that people were splashing in, jumping through and just lounging in. Ah, now I understood why they called it a pool party. Hm.

"Yo, Loch!"

I turned my head to see a Loch clone staring intensely at us standing to our left in a group of hot guys interspersed with hot girls.

"Hey, Ryke," Loch replied. He leaned down to my ear as we walked toward the guy. "Ryker's my brother."

Holy crap. Ryker had grown up nicely. He was missing the cuteness and easygoing demeanor that Loch had but he was still very handsome in spite of what I'd soon learn was an aloof manner.

When we got to him, Ryker questioned, "You talk to Dad?"

"Not today, why? Oh, this is Celeste. Celeste, my brother Ryker."

"Hi," I said, giving Ryker a smile.

His eyes narrowed as he looked my way then he jerked his chin up at me, but when he continued staring at me as he talked, I grew uncomfortable. "Shop got vandalized last night. Bunch of thugs got in the back fence and fucked some shit up. Needs us to come by tomorrow and help sort shit out."

"I've told him he needed lights with motion sensors back there at the very least. Any real damage?"

Ryker didn't answer but kept looking at me for a moment before he stated, "I know you."

I felt my heart pounding in my chest and I was starting to sweat. Shit! (Yes, this was definitely a time for cussing).

"Celeste used to live here when she was little. Maybe you saw her in school? What school'd you go to?" Loch asked me.

"Uh, Stevens Elementary," I responded, my voice shaky under Ryker's watchful stare.

"See, Ryke? That's probably it. That's where we went," Loch suggested.

"Hm," Ryker muttered. As he continued to focus on me, I suddenly saw a spark of recognition on his face which was when my eyes got huge and I held my breath because I knew he knew I was the brat who, when Loch and I were seven, had helped hide his video game controller. He remained watching me for a moment, that stone face of his about to make my heart jump out of my chest, then he squinted as if he was trying to figure out my game and I saw him purse his lips. Then it was over and he looked at Loch. "Yeah, well, make sure you're at the shop tomorrow at eight a.m."

"Christ. Dad know we've got lives?"

"Right now Dad doesn't give a fuck. He needs us, we're there." I sucked in my breath when Ryker nodded at me, letting me know he was on to me, then he turned and walked away. When I was in the clear, stupid me then puffed out what was left in my lungs then gulped in so much air I had to cough a couple times.

"You okay?" Loch asked.

"Yeah," I said raspily. "Might need a drink."

"On it," he answered and led us to one of the many kegs, grabbing us a couple cups.

"Thank you," I said before guzzling it down. Better. I looked around at the chaos. "Um, how is this party legal when it's on campus?"

"It's not. On campus that is. Technically, the land is owned by the guy who had all this built. Wouldn't say it's legal but most of the campus cops turn a blind eye to it every year since it's so close to the dorms and not many people drink and drive, I guess." He shrugged then took my hand leading me toward the football field. "This is where shit gets real."

Once we got down there, I saw how real things got. There were pools all over the field, some bigger than others and some that didn't have water in them but other things like mud and Jell-O and girls were wrestling in them. Uh.

"Loch!" we heard someone holler and turning to see who it was, I saw a guy grinning at him then I heard Loch answer, "Fuck yeah!" The next thing I knew I was being dragged behind him heading to the monstrous slide where a group of guys who'd gone down it had to tell Loch how badass it was.

Before I could get anything out, you know, like protest maybe, he bent to take off my shoes, pull my coverup over my head, put me in front of him at the steps, said, "Climb, baby," and then we were at the top. What in the effity eff was I doing?

I turned to him, eyes huge. "Uh, Loch, it's pretty high. I don't know—"

"C'mon! It'll be fun!" Then I was sitting in front of him, his legs at either side of mine, one arm around my waist, then he pushed off with the other and all I could do was scream. The whole way down.

"How fucking fun was that?" he declared looking like a little boy who'd gotten exactly what he'd wanted on Christmas morning. He leaned down and touched his lips to mine then hollered, "Let's do it again!" pulled me up, and there we went again.

Three more times later, I'd had enough. "Loch, if we go again, I'm gonna have to have my bottoms surgically removed from the perpetual wedgie I'm getting," I groaned at which he died laughing watching as I tugged on them.

"I'd be glad to help," he responded with a grin and I swear he mumbled, "with my teeth," but I couldn't be sure and really didn't want to ask.

We stopped by a pool that had water and ice in it and Loch fished a couple cans of beer out for us, opening mine before handing it to me so I wouldn't "break a nail."

Okay, where was the asshole who'd humiliated me all those years ago? The guy who'd shamed Samantha for getting the free lunch or stood up Mary at the homeless shelter? The jerk who outted Marcy in her quest to have boobs? Nowhere to be seen, that's where, so I made a decision.

There were portable toilets (yuck) all over the place and I needed to call Marcy to tell her the jig was up, so I excused myself from Loch and headed to the nearest free potty. It wasn't so bad inside since the party had just started but I could only imagine its nastiness at night's end. I shuddered at the thought as I closed the door and locked it then pulled my phone out of my pocket.

"How's it going?" Marcy's voice was full of curiosity when she answered.

"Not well. I can't do this anymore, Marce. He's changed."

I heard a *pfftt* sound come out of her mouth. "Whatever. He's just being charming because you're new. Wait until he gets tired of you then he'll be up to his old tricks again."

"Thanks?" I muttered.

"The guy's an asshole. You know it. I know it. People don't change."

"But they mature," I pointed out.

"Yeah, well, I'll believe it when I see it."

"How can you see it if I don't even give him a chance?"

"Your call, Sim. But when he pulls his shit, don't think I won't tell you I told you so."

I sighed. "All right. Are you having fun?"

"Yes! Isn't this the craziest thing?"

I chuckled. "Pretty crazy. Okay, I'll talk to you tonight?"

"Pretty sure I'm staying at Adam's!" I had to pull the phone away from my ear at her squeal.

"Ah, so I see Operation W… H… S… um… F-T Squared is working out."

"Operation W-H Squared what?"

"We're Having Sex for the First Time," I explained.

I heard her snort. "Yes! We are! God, you computer majors are so analytical and literal in your thinking."

"And Triple C was my idea?"

Now she laughed. "Touché. All right, I'll talk to you tomorrow, okay?"

"Gotcha. Have fun!"

We hung up and I left the toilet having made my mind up that I was going to tell Loch who I really was and I'd just have to deal with the consequences.

And if that meant he wanted me gone, so be it.

Confession Number Five

As I made my way back through the crowd I could see the top of Loch's head since he stood so tall, probably around six-two or so, and when I got closer, I saw that he wasn't alone and he was having what looked like a very heated discussion with a pretty blond girl and she was crying. Oh no. I stopped and stood-slash-hid behind a humongous guy who was downing the contents of a beer bong and waited for the girl to leave not wanting to intrude (although I was definitely spying but whatever).

"Like I've told you for the past month, Kinzie, no fuckin' way. I'm done with you. Now leave me the fuck alone," I heard Loch hiss then I saw the girl turn with a sob and run away.

Well, crap! He really was still a jerk. Triple C back on. I felt the walls I'd just let down move back in place as I stepped out from behind Gigantor and went to where Loch was.

"Everything okay?" I asked.

His head shot around and for just a moment he looked at me like I'd just caught him with his hand in the cookie jar. Then he put his hands on my hips. "Yeah. It's good. Dated her a couple months ago, but she's a fuckin' liar. Tried acting like she was someone she wasn't and I found out. Hate that shit. I ended it but she's still holdin' on."

I felt all the blood leave my face as I looked at him. Fruckity fruckin' fruck! The only way the evening could end now was with Loch hating me because I was exactly the girl he'd just described. Damn it!

Suddenly his eyes got intense on mine and he looked a bit like Ryker for a second which was kind of scary. "Come on," he said, grabbing my hand and pulling me behind him through the crowd and out toward the field.

When we got there, I saw that there weren't just swimming pools set up everywhere but there was a giant plastic tarp put down and it was being used as a mammoth Slip and Slide. I watched as a group of clearly drunk guys, maybe seven of them, did a countdown then they all ran up to the thing and flinging themselves down on it, slid nearly thirty yards before either coming to a gradual stop or careening off the side into the grass for a nice turf burn. Good grief.

And we were headed that way. Oh, heck no.

"Uh, we're not doing that, are we?" I squeaked out.

Loch's hand gripped mine harder when I tried pulling mine from his but when we passed right by the tarp of torture and kept going I can't even explain the relief I felt. As we rounded what looked like some kind of fieldhouse, I wondered what we were doing until he pressed me against the wall with his body flush against mine then our lips collided when he bent to give me a bruising kiss.

Oh my word.

As the kiss grew hotter, Loch got really aggressive then, sticking his knee between my legs to where his thigh rubbed against my center, or maybe I was the one doing the rubbing, who knew at this point, then his hand slid down and under my cover-up where he clutched my bottom jerking me closer to him. And, Jesus Christ on ice, I knew I should've called it off but then amazingly, the kiss got even deeper. Frick! But damn it, I was all in, totally understanding his urgency right then because we definitely had crazy chemistry going on between us, which I'd already unabashedly exhibited on my porch earlier.

When one of his hands moved to my breast cupping it, his thumb gliding over my straining nipple, I moaned right into his mouth, loud and needy and all *I want you and I don't care if you stomped all over my heart before and even if you're still a jerk, just do me, do me now!* Then things got even wilder, if you can believe it, which was when he grabbed my leg, hitching it over his hip and began grinding against me.

And God help me but I wanted him. Wanted him right there! When my hands went to the front of his board shorts searching for a way to get them off, that's when I finally got it together.

Tearing my mouth from his and pushing him back, I stood looking up at him as my breaths came fast. He was breathing just as heavily and his dark eyes on mine told me he wanted me just as badly as I did him but this was crazy and had to stop! We didn't even know each other! I mean, I knew *who* he was, knew he was probably still a jerk, but this was going way too fast (not to mention the fact that I'd almost pantsed him in public).

"Loch," I whispered.

"Celeste," he whispered back and at that moment, I really hated that Triple C was going on because I'd have loved to hear him say my first name in that raspy voice of his right then.

But good gosh! I had to be careful here because if I wasn't, I'd end up sleeping with him tonight and what a mess that would be. Then I wanted to smack myself because I actually started considering it, sleeping with him, trying to convince myself that would be a heck of a way to *really* get back at him. Like, maybe teasing him with some serious foreplay back at my place then asking him to leave. Or going so far as giving him an amazing blow job and pulling away when he got close and making him beg me to finish him before I kicked him out. Or, what the hell, how about just screwing his brains out until we were both exhausted, having had the best sex of our lives, before I owned up to everything and he stormed out because I was a big fat liar.

Yeah, all those scenarios were just fantastic with me playing the part of a deceitful, evil skank. And it'd be especially fantastic when he *told people* afterward that I was a deceitful, evil skank. And it'd be even worse when he himself believed I was those things.

Ugh.

This had to end. Even if he was still a jerk, there obviously was something between us that neither of us could deny and I needed to confess to my wicked scheme right now before things went too far.

So taking a deep breath then letting it out, I bit my lips for a moment before deciding to be a grown up and tell him. "Loch?"

"Right here, babe," he answered, the gold flecks in his eyes seeming to radiate warmly as he looked down at me.

God.

"I need to te—"

"Powers! What's up, bro?" a guy called from behind us.

I turned to see two guys and two girls behind us.

"What's up, Olly?" Loch said and he and the two dudes did that handshake shoulder bump thing that guys did.

"Heading to my folks' place where there's a real pool. You should come," the Olly guy declared, looking at me letting me know I was invited too.

Loch put his arm around my shoulders then tilting his head to the side toward me said to his friends, "This is Celeste. Celeste, this is Neal Oliver and his girlfriend Regan Reed." Neal or Olly, gave me a chin lift and Regan smiled and said hi. "And this is Ky Fisher and his girlfriend Julie Owens." The second couple greeted me the same and I returned the greeting.

"Whaddya say? You coming?" Olly asked.

Loch looked down at me, eyebrows up. "Yeah?"

"Uh, sure. If you want," I replied, gazing up at him with a small smile and his arm around my shoulders squeezed me in affirmation. Then he leaned down to brush his lips to mine before we followed the other two couples off the football field and we went to his truck.

And I just kept getting in deeper.

~*~*~*~

"You went to Cal?" Julie asked from where she sat across from me in the hot tub. All three of us girls sat in the Jacuzzi while the guys goofed around in the pool playing a game of HORSE with a floating basketball goal and ball.

"Yeah, for two years," I responded then took a drink from my beer bottle.

"That's awesome!" she responded. "I have a friend who went there this year."

"Oh, yeah?"

"Yep. He's crazy. Said he wants to be the next 'Naked Guy' walking around campus, and knowing him, well, I'll probably be seeing him on CNN soon." She snorted.

I laughed. "He'll fit right in. Some of the people there are pretty radical. Within my first hour of being on campus freshman year I'd been offered pot, asked to hug a tree and then a guy begged me to sign a petition to save the penis snake, which I thought he was being creepy but it's actually a real snake."

Julie and Regan laughed with me. I really liked them. They were both friendly and funny and I was glad to meet new people even though once they found out what I was doing to Loch they'd probably hate me.

"So how'd you meet Loch?" Regan asked. "I think he's just the sweetest thing ever, always so nice to everyone," she said in her southern accent. I'd found out that she was from Georgia and had come to Hallervan on a volleyball scholarship.

She thought he was the sweetest thing ever? And nice to everyone? I mean, I'd gotten a glimpse of that but it still didn't erase all he'd done when he was younger, did it?

"I, uh, met him in class Wednesday," I explained.

"He *is* very nice," Julie chimed in. "My friend Madi is really self-conscious about her weight and decided to take a weight lifting class last year. She said Loch was one of the student aides and was so sweet to her, helping her find a routine that worked for her. She lost thirty pounds because of him!"

I looked over at Loch who, beer in one hand and the basketball in the other, stood about six feet from the side of the pool. He took off running toward the water and jumped in the air, spinning around and throwing the ball over his head at the basket before he made a huge splash. When he came up out of the water, the two other guys were throwing a fit because he'd made the shot then they were all laughing and shouting at each other in disbelief and I had to chuckle.

And now I was more than confused. Was he a nice guy? Was he an ass? I couldn't decide anymore. But what I did decide was I had to end whatever it was we had between us, no matter how attracted we were to each other or how much I found I liked him. It just wasn't fair to him since I'd gone into this planning on hurting him.

And the brilliant part of it? I wouldn't even have to tell him who I really was. I'd just make a clean break of it and move on.

So yep. That's what I'd do. End it. No matter how chickenshit my plan was.

As I was mulling this over there was a splash in the hot tub as the guys all jumped in then Loch was there beside me.

"Hey, baby," he said, leaning in and touching his lips to mine.

"Hey," I answered softly as he sat then pulled me to sit sideways in his lap.

Let me just say right now, Loch Powers with his shirt off was a motherfrickin' sight to behold. Sweet Mary, his was definitely a body to cuss about. The man had abs for days and pecs and biceps and lord have mercy, tattoos. When we'd gotten to Neal's (or Olly's) parents' house and come out back to get in the pool and Loch had taken off his t-shirt, well, I think my chin hit my chest since my mouth was hanging open so big. And now I was on his lap and everything was on full display for my viewing pleasure and, boy, did I view.

"Having fun?" he asked.

"Yeah. I like your friends," I whispered back and saw him smile before he pressed his lips to mine for a sweet kiss. When he pulled back, I looked down at his chest examining his tattoos. Pointing at a smallish four-leaf clover just below his clavicle on his right side I inquired, "Any significance for this one other than luck?"

He tucked his chin to look where I was pointing. "I got it because I *am* a lucky sonuvabitch," he returned with a grin, squeezing my right butt cheek where his hand was resting. I jumped a bit which made him laugh. "Oh, and I'm Irish." He winked at me.

I smiled. "This one?" I touched my finger to his right pec that was covered with a clock that was breaking apart.

He shrugged. "It means a couple things. To remind me that life is short and to live every second of it. Also that time heals all wounds."

I moved my hand down to his side where what looked like a Spanish phrase was tattooed. My eyes came to his and I raised my eyebrows.

"Movie line."

"From *Road House*?" I asked, eyebrows still raised.

He threw his head back and laughed and I felt my chest squeeze because it was possibly the most amazing thing I'd ever seen.

Crap.

I really was getting in way too deep with him but I didn't know how to stop it. He just kept drawing me in and I just kept not resisting. Damn it!

His head came back and his eyes twinkled as they lit on mine. "No, baby. It's from *Butch Cassidy and the Sundance Kid*." When my eyebrows still remained up, he shook his head. "You haven't seen it either?" At my own head shake, he sighed. "Gonna have to have Movie Night with you soon." The thrill that went through me upon hearing that should've had me getting off his lap and asking him to take me home. But nope. Stupid me couldn't resist hearing what he had to say, thus digging myself a deeper hole with him which of course only made me like him more. "Okay. Last scene when they're holed up and surrounded by, like, the entire fuckin' Bolivian army. Right before they go out Butch asks Sundance if he saw this lawman named Lefors, who's been chasing them forever, out there." He tucked a piece of hair behind my ear then went on. "Sundance looks worried but tells Butch no, he hasn't seen Lefors. They don't realize how many armed men are waiting to shoot them, so it's kinda funny, ironic, that he asks if this lone man is waiting to get them. Anyway, my tattoo is Butch's last line, 'Oh good. For a moment there, I thought we were in trouble.'"

Hm. That was a bit odd. "Why Spanish?" I queried.

He lifted a shoulder. "Why not? They're in Bolivia." Then he grinned.

I just stared at him. Then I blinked trying to process why he'd want this on his body.

"Reminds me to be aware, babe. Stay on my toes and not get fuckin' duped, you know?"

Shit.

Shit shit shit.

I was such a slimy, duping bitch for the plan I'd made tonight and it made me feel horrible.

But I nodded anyway, ever the con artist, ducking my head in shame but when I did this, I saw the tattoo over his heart.

"*The Little Prince*," I mumbled, running my finger over the words that were branded there. "'I was too young to know how to love her,'" I read then looked at him in question and saw his face flush in embarrassment. What in the world? "What's this one?"

"Tell you later," he said quietly, running his nose along my jaw then back toward my neck where he nuzzled into me making me shiver.

"Okay," I whispered, my mouth at his ear which offered a sudden temptation, so blaming the four beers I'd had since getting there (and my supreme stupidity), I took his earlobe lightly between my teeth and tugged a little which got me a horse bite from him on my neck making me tuck my neck to my shoulder with a giggle and pull away.

And sweet Jesus, the look on his face. Good Christ, the man could seduce me with that alone, a half smirk tipping one side of his mouth up and his eyes piercing mine with a promise of many good things to come and I felt my stomach dip in a really, really good way.

Oh my.

"You ready to go?" he said softly and I nodded. He lifted me off his lap then we stood and got out of the hot tub and dried off. Before we left, I exchanged phone numbers with Julie and Regan knowing we'd probably never be friends (which made me sad), then Loch took my hand and led me out.

In the truck on the way back, he still held my hand, resting the back of his on the console as he stroked his thumb against the back of mine. We didn't talk the whole way and I swear there was so much sexual tension in his truck cab that it was almost hard to breathe. When we pulled up to my house, I saw there were no lights on and assumed Marcy had stayed with Adam and I wondered if I should invite Loch in knowing it'd only lead to trouble but wanting to all the same. Then I remembered I had to tell him we were through.

We sat there for several moments, me biting my lip as I stared out the windshield wondering why I'd agreed to go through with Triple C in the first place and knowing when Loch found out who I was, he'd hate me. I was having an entire conversation in my head about it all, going back and forth getting my goodbye speech ready when I felt a tug on my hand.

"What's going on in that pretty head?" Loch queried when I looked over at him.

God. So handsome. So freaking hot.

As I took a deep breath I was glad I'd had a few beers to relax me because I'm sure I would've been flipping out right about then if not. So after taking another breath and blowing it out, I decided to spill. "I need to tell you something." I glanced over at him about to bite through my lip I was so nervous.

"You can tell me whatever you want, babe." He reached his hand out and cupped my chin then ran his thumb over my bottom lip gently pulling it out from my teeth then his hand slid to the back of my neck and he pulled me in for a kiss.

And it wasn't just any kiss. It was one of the hottest kisses I'd ever had. It started out soft, our tongues almost lazily twisting together. But then Loch ramped it up, his hand getting tighter at the back of my head, his fingers clenching in my hair, the movement of our tongues getting wilder, desperate even, and just through that kiss alone I knew exactly what he wanted from me which wasn't far off from what I knew I shouldn't want from him.

When he pulled back, he looked me right in the eyes and stated, "Wanna do things to you I probably shouldn't be wanting to do right now, babe." And all the wind was practically knocked out of me. Holy crap. Then he continued. "But seeing as this is our first date and you're probably worried I'd think you were easy or something," he grinned at me now which made me want to kiss him more, "I'll leave it at this." He leaned in and took my mouth with his again and frack me if it wasn't hotter than the previous kiss.

When he pulled away, all I could do was sit there, my brain scrambled and I was breathing so heavily I knew I was fogging up his windows. He winked at me then got out of the truck and came around to help me out. When we got to the front door, he reached into the pocket of my cover-up for my keys and somehow guessing correctly, put the correct key in the door and unlocked it.

We stood there for a second before I came out of my daze. "Thank you," I whispered. "I had a great time tonight."

He smiled down at me. "I did too. What're you doing tomorrow night?"

"I don't think—" I began but he cut me off.

He put his forehead against mine. "I wanna see you again."

Still, I tried to stay my ground. "Loch, it's probably not—"

His lips covered mine as he mumbled against them, "Wanna see you, Celeste."

"I, uh, I have to work. But I get off at nine," I pulled away and blurted.

This got me a grin then we were kissing again, hard and deep and wet and hot and when he moved away my head was spinning.

"I'll call you," he said quietly and bent to brush his lips against mine one last time which ended too abruptly and I hated that because I think I could've stayed lip-locked to him all night long. He smirked at me then opened the door and handed me the keys. "Goodnight, Celeste."

I stared up at him, wondering how the heck he'd manipulated me so easily into going out with him again. I also knew there was something I was supposed to do but I couldn't wrap my brain around anything but wanting to kiss him again, so I tiptoed up and touched my lips to his. "Thank you."

"Go," he said when I went flat-footed and nodded toward my door.

Normally, his bossiness would've made me balk but I only remarked, "Okay. 'Night," and went inside, giving him a shy smile as I kept looking at him, moving my head with the door as I slowly closed it then locked it.

I walked to my room with what was probably a goofy smile and plopped down on my bed, my head hitting the pillow as I let out a dreamy sigh.

Loch Powers was the sexiest man I'd ever seen. Holy hell, I could so easily fall for him. Goofy smile number two flashed across my face as I thought about how sweet he was.

It wasn't when I got up and put on my pjs, brushed my teeth, made my way back to my room and with another winsome sigh landed on my bed thinking that falling for someone was always the best part of a relationship that I got my head straight. Nope, it was just as I closed my eyes that I realized I'd totally blown Triple C and the end game of telling Loch we were over.

My eyes flew open and I cringed.

Shit.

Confession Number Six

As I lay there berating myself, my phone buzzed but when I saw it was Loch I grinned like a flippin' schoolgirl.

What was wrong with me?

Text Message—Sat, Aug. 16, 12:39 a.m.

Assface: I miss your lips...

But, oh, my God, how sweet was that? I immediately went about changing his name in my phone because "Assface" just wasn't appropriate anymore. Then my brain started making rationalizations about the whole situation. We were attracted to each other. People who were attracted to each other did things together all the time. What harm would it be if I saw him again?

Okay. New decision. I'd go out with him one more time then I'd break things off with him. I could handle that, right? So feeling all giddy inside at this new resolution, I proceeded to answer him.

Text Message—Sat, Aug. 16, 12:39 a.m.

Me: Would it help if I told you I feel the same?

Text Message—Sat, Aug. 16, 12:40 a.m.

Loch: Helps but doesn't solve anything ;)

Text Message—Sat, Aug. 16, 12:40 a.m.

Me: lol true

Text Message—Sat, Aug. 16, 12:40 a.m.

Loch: So, tomorrow...

> Text Message—Sat, Aug. 16, 12:40 a.m.
>
> Me: Yes?

> Text Message—Sat, Aug. 16, 12:41 a.m.
>
> Loch: How about Movie Night at my place?

Another thrill ran through my body making me shiver at the thought of seeing him again. The dip in my womb let me know that I couldn't wait to have his lips on mine again. Oh man. I was in serious trouble.

> Text Message—Sat, Aug. 16, 12:41 a.m.
>
> Me: I'd like that a lot :)

Can you tell I was *so* concerned about the trouble I was in?

> Text Message—Sat, Aug. 16, 12:41 a.m.
>
> Loch: Pick you up at 9:30?

> Text Message—Sat, Aug. 16, 12:42 a.m.
>
> Me: If you give me directions to your place, I can just drive there after work

> Text Message—Sat, Aug. 16, 12:42 a.m.
>
> Loch: I can do that, baby

And him calling me baby? Holy crap. That was so hot too!

> Text Message—Sat, Aug. 16, 12:42 a.m.
>
> Me: Okay :)

> Text Message—Sat, Aug. 16, 12:42 a.m.
>
> Loch: Can I ask you something?

Text Message—Sat, Aug. 16, 12:42 a.m.

Me: Sure

I sat up quickly waiting to see what he'd text, my stomach in knots knowing that when he'd gotten home Ryker had probably told him he knew who I was. Shit!

Text Message—Sat, Aug. 16, 12:43 a.m.

Loch: What're you wearing?

The mother of all exhalations left my body and I fell back onto my bed. Frack!

How did spies and double agents do this crap, being all duplicitous and stuff because I seriously sucked at it. I breathed more easily as I replied, relieved that Ryker hadn't spilled the beans but still feeling bad about the dilemma I was in.

Text Message—Sat, Aug. 16, 12:43 a.m.

Me: Guys are such visual creatures… or is perv the word I'm looking for?

Text Message—Sat, Aug. 16, 12:43 a.m.

Loch: Baby, you can call me whatever you want, I just wanna know what you've got on

Text Message—Sat, Aug. 16, 12:43 a.m.

Me: Why?

Text Message—Sat, Aug. 16, 12:43 a.m.

Loch: So when I jack off to thoughts of you here in a minute it'll help me see you better

Oh, my damn! Another womb dip bombarded me as my breath caught.

Holy gah!

Obviously I wasn't feeling too bad about the way the evening had turned out because I was thoroughly enjoying this.

Man, I was one sick and twisted woman.

Text Message—Sat, Aug. 16, 12:44 a.m.

Me: Loch…

Text Message—Sat, Aug. 16, 12:44 a.m.

Loch: Babe… tell me

Text Message—Sat, Aug. 16, 12:44 a.m.

Me: A UDub t-shirt that was my brother's

Text Message—Sat, Aug. 16, 12:44 a.m.

Loch: Panties?

Yikes!

Text Message—Sat, Aug. 16, 12:45 a.m.

Me: Yes…

Text Message—Sat, Aug. 16, 12:45 a.m.

Loch: Color?

Holy crap. The man *really* needed a visual. And was I really going to give him spank bank material? Yes. Yes, I was. Ack!

Text Message—Sat, Aug. 16, 12:45 a.m.

Me: Um... it's kind of embarrassing

Text Message—Sat, Aug. 16, 12:45 a.m.

Loch: Tell me

Text Message—Sat, Aug. 16, 12:45 a.m.

Me: They're kind of funny

Text Message—Sat, Aug. 16, 12:46 a.m.

Loch: Babe, now

Text Message—Sat, Aug. 16, 12:46 a.m.

Me: Wow, bossy much?

Text Message—Sat, Aug. 16, 12:46 a.m.

Loch: Tell me

Text Message—Sat, Aug. 16, 12:46 a.m.

Me: It's embarrassing

Text Message—Sat, Aug. 16, 12:46 a.m.

Loch: NOW

Text Message—Sat, Aug. 16, 12:46 a.m.

Me: Persistent, aren't you? What're YOU wearing? HUH?

Text Message—Sat, Aug. 16, 12:47 a.m.

Loch: Nothing

Holy jeez! Now *that* was a visual!

Text Message—Sat, Aug. 16, 12:47 a.m.

Loch: Tell me or I'm coming over to see for myself

Text Message—Sat, Aug. 16, 12:47 a.m.

Me: No!

Text Message—Sat, Aug. 16, 12:47 a.m.

Loch: On my way

Text Message—Sat, Aug. 16, 12:47 a.m.

Me: Okay, jeez! They're Victoria's Secret tiger striped ones that say "Roar" on the butt. Happy now?

I winced as I covered my face with my hand. Boy, a little peer pressure and I told all.

Text Message—Sat, Aug. 16, 12:48 a.m.

Loch: Extremely happy. Now, was that so bad?

Text Message—Sat, Aug. 16, 12:48 a.m.

Me: No but it was embarrassing

Text Message—Sat, Aug. 16, 12:48 a.m.

Loch: Babe. Gotta learn to be open with me. I wanna get to know you better. I wanna know everything about you

If he only knew how little time he had.

Text Message—Sat, Aug. 16, 12:48 a.m.

Me: Okay. Will you tell me about The Little Prince tattoo?

Text Message—Sat, Aug. 16, 12:49 a.m.

Loch: Gotta promise not to get mad, yeah?

Text Message—Sat, Aug. 16, 12:49 a.m.

Me: Yeah...

I thought about his tattoo. *I was too young to know how to love her*. Was he still in love with someone from his past? Great.

Text Message—Sat, Aug. 16, 12:49 a.m.

Loch: There was this girl

Yep. Here we went.

Text Message—Sat, Aug. 16, 12:49 a.m.

Loch: We grew up together. She was beautiful. She was also my best friend. And then she wasn't.

Wait. What?

Text Message—Sat, Aug. 16, 12:50 a.m.

Loch: I have to tell you, I was a real asshole when I was younger and I was mean to her

Text Message—Sat, Aug. 16, 12:50 a.m.

Me: Mean how?

Text Message—Sat, Aug. 16, 12:50 a.m.

Loch: I just did stupid shit like ignore her because I thought I was so fucking cool. One of the last times I talked to her, I was really rude

Oh, my God. My chest got tight and I wanted to think he was talking about me but I didn't know if that was just my ego talking. Marcy had said he'd been mean to a lot of girls.

Text Message—Sat, Aug. 16, 12:51 a.m.

Loch: She moved before I could apologize. I can still see the look on her face. Told myself if I ever saw her again I'd set shit right but doubt I'll ever get the chance. She probably fucking hates me anyway. I was pretty mean. Got the tattoo to remind me of her… and not to be a dick.

Damn! Why hadn't I just told him who I was?

Text Message—Sat, Aug. 16, 12:51 a.m.

Loch: Not that I'm in love with her or anything but I'd like to tell her I'm sorry. But she's probably some psycho bitch now who's gonna hunt me down and make me pay for humiliating her or some shit lol

Uh.

Text Message—Sat, Aug. 16, 12:51 a.m.

Me: Well…

Text Message—Sat, Aug. 16, 12:51 a.m.

Loch: You think it's dumb

Text Message—Sat, Aug. 16, 12:51 a.m.

Me: No, I don't!

Text Message—Sat, Aug. 16, 12:52 a.m.

Loch: So that's the story behind it. Make sense?

It did. But then a thought came to me. What if he was talking about Samantha Hays? He'd embarrassed her about getting a free lunch when her dad had been laid off and then she'd moved to another school. And she'd been beautiful and I knew I hadn't been anywhere close to beautiful when I was that age. I was hit with a wave of depression knowing he was probably talking about her and not me.

Text Message—Sat, Aug. 16, 12:52 a.m.

Me: Yes, it does

Text Message—Sat, Aug. 16, 12:52 a.m.

Loch: You good?

Text Message—Sat, Aug. 16, 12:52 a.m.

Me: I'm good.

Text Message—Sat, Aug. 16, 12:52 a.m.

Loch: Tomorrow night, okay?

Text Message—Sat, Aug. 16, 12:53 a.m.

Me: Okay

Text Message—Sat, Aug. 16, 12:53 a.m.

Loch: I'll text you my address, yeah?

Text Message—Sat, Aug. 16, 12:53 a.m.

Me: Yeah

Text Message—Sat, Aug. 16, 12:53 a.m.

Loch: Look, I like you a lot. You're beautiful, intelligent, sweet, funny, hot... I didn't mean to embarrass you earlier. You're safe with me, you know

And there it was. He was being sweet again.

Text Message—Sat, Aug. 16, 12:53 a.m.

Me: Okay, Loch

Text Message—Sat, Aug. 16, 12:54 a.m.

Loch: Talk to you tomorrow?

> Text Message—Sat, Aug. 16, 12:54 a.m.
>
> **Me: Okay**
>
> Text Message—Sat, Aug. 16, 12:54 a.m.
>
> **Loch: Have sweet dreams**
>
> Text Message—Sat, Aug. 16, 12:54 a.m.
>
> **Me: You too**
>
> Text Message—Sat, Aug. 16, 12:54 a.m.
>
> **Loch: I will… especially knowing what you've got on… fuckin' hot, babe ;)**

I face-palmed myself again. How in the world had I gotten in this mess? I felt horrible flirting with him because of the big fat lie I'd spun and now knowing that he was pining for Samantha Hays I felt like a fool. Just brilliant.

> Text Message—Sat, Aug. 16, 12:54 a.m.
>
> **Me: Night, Loch**
>
> Text Message—Sat, Aug. 16, 12:55 a.m.
>
> **Loch: Night, baby xx**

I set my phone on my nightstand angry that I hadn't come clean with him from the beginning. Why hadn't I just told him who I was and what a prick he'd been when we were younger and maybe he would've apologized and we could've started over. But nooooo, I had to keep things under wraps then weave this stupid web of lies that I'd never get out of unscathed.

Turning on my side I put my hand under my pillow and curled my knees up in my typical falling to sleep position. And just as I was drifting off, I hoped that he hadn't been talking about Samantha and wanting to find her. I also hoped that when I told him I couldn't see him anymore, he'd understand.

But I doubted he would.

~*~*~*~

"So how'd it go last night?" Marcy asked when I emerged from my room around nine the next morning.

Cripes. I hadn't expected her to be home that early and my stumbling over my own feet proved it. I'd only gotten up early for a Saturday because we all know a guilty conscience won't let you sleep and wasn't I the lucky one.

"Uh..." I offered.

She spooned her cereal into her mouth and remarked, "You didn't do it, did you?"

I pulled the Pop-Tarts box from the cabinet proceeding to open the package then the wrapper and put them in the toaster, a bit annoyed at my failure to perform Triple C last night. Really, I think I was just annoyed at Triple C itself. But as I stood watching the toaster taking its sweet time, I found I was actually annoyed at everything. Turning to get the milk out of the fridge I poured myself a glass and stated grumpily to Marcy, "I told you I wasn't going to do it."

I took a drink and over the top of my glass saw her shrug indifferently which made me even grouchier because she was the one who'd come up with the plan in the first place. A plan I hadn't wanted to execute from the start. Jeez. So Afraid I'd say something rude, I turned back to the toaster and waited for my pastries to pop up. Eight billion years later, they were done and I placed them on a paper towel then went to sit at the table.

We sat in silence for a while before I shared quietly, "I really like him, Marce."

I watched as she leaned back in her chair, closing her eyes and sighing. She then opened her eyes and canted her head to the side to look at me. "Has he really changed?"

I shrugged. "I think he has. He was so nice to me last night. He was nice to everyone. And he's a really, really good kisser." I took a bite of the deliciousness that was frosted Pop-Tarts, barely holding back a groan.

I saw a smirk appear on her face as she watched at me. "Of course he is. He's a Powers. They're supposedly all sex gods." She wasn't lying with that statement but I snorted when she rolled her eyes after saying it.

"I'm, um, supposed to go to his place tonight to watch movies."

She sat up and pushed her bowl to the side, clasping her hands on the table and leaning on her forearms raising her eyebrows at me. "I guess that means you're gonna get laid then, huh?"

"Marcy!" I snapped. "I don't even know him!"

"So?"

"So? So I don't sleep with guys I don't know!" Kissed their face off and practically humped their leg, but sex? No!

Jesus, I was ridiculous.

"You've never had a one-night stand?"

"No." I narrowed my eyes at her. She knew this about me but I could see she was holding back. "Why're you grinning? What! You've had one?"

She nodded. "Jeff Marshall. Senior year."

"Shut up! He was, like, the second hottest guy in class next to Loch!"

"At Tad Dillard's party right before graduation. Knew I didn't want a relationship with him because he's at Florida playing football now and the whole long-distance shit wasn't for me. But, yep, I nailed him."

"Holy cow," I muttered kind of in awe of my best friend.

"He called for three weeks straight. Tried walking me to class for two. But I told him it wouldn't work. And holy crap, he was such an alpha, so pushy and bossy, which was great during the sex, and I almost gave in and dated him since he wouldn't take no for an answer but figured it wouldn't go anywhere so I stuck to my guns." I thought I saw some regret in her face. Hm. "I dated a guy, Anthony, from UDub last year who was like that. Straight alpha. Bossy. Pushy. Amazing at sex. Best six months of my life."

I wanted to laugh at the faraway look she got but then I realized something.

"Loch's like that," I relayed, my eyes big thinking about how he'd been bossy last night.

She came out of her fog then said with a chuckle, "I thought he would be."

"That's part of the reason I didn't get to tell him. It was like he knew how he wanted everything to go and then made it happen. Come to think of it, he kind of railroaded me into seeing him tonight."

"Better watch out then 'cause before you know it, you'll be under the covers with him and you'll have no idea how you got there. But you'll love it." She got that wistful look in her eyes again.

What she said made me think. Could I be comfortable sleeping with Loch tonight even though we didn't really know each other? No, I didn't think I could.

"I know it sounds old-fashioned, but I think you have to know the person, care about them, to give your body to them." She raised an eyebrow. "Don't get me wrong! One-night stands have their place. I get it if that's all someone wants. I'm just saying I'd want more with Loch, that's all. Is that weird?"

"Not weird at all. I understand."

"But, man, I'd love to bang him." This made her crack up. I smiled too. "It's been a long time since I got laid. Jared and I broke up last April and since we hadn't been together for a month before that," I counted on my fingers, "I'm going on six months of no sex, and Loch had me so hot and bothered last night that I don't know if I can keep from jumping his bones if I go tonight." Crap.

"So you told him who you really are then?"

My hand stopped in midair as I was leading the Pop-Tart to my mouth to give myself another mouth-gasm and I grimaced when I looked at her. "Uh, not yet."

That got her attention and she bit off, "What?"

I shook my head as I chewed, the pastry in my mouth now tasting like cardboard.

"Sim! What the hell? How's this gonna work?"

I winced because I was as clueless as she was. "I don't know." I heard her scoff then I quickly continued. "But I planned on calling it all off tonight."

"You're ending it tonight? Would that be before or after you sleep with him? Because you will sleep with him if he's anything like Anthony."

"I don't know," I whispered with a frown, not liking how muddled my thinking was.

"Wait. Are you even gonna tell him who you are before you leave?"

I guess the look on my face answered her question.

She threw up her hands. "You've got to be kidding. You tell me you really like him but instead of coming clean, you're gonna sleep with the guy then tell him you can't see him anymore without his ever knowing who you are."

I kept looking at her.

"I've always thought you were pretty smart but this plan is pure idiocy, Sim. You don't think he's eventually gonna find out who you are?"

Crap. I hadn't thought of that. "Crap."

"Yeah, crap. Who the hell are you right now?"

"I don't know," I whispered again.

She shook her head as she got up to rinse her bowl out and put it in the dishwasher. "Look, thinking about it, I know Triple C was kinda messed up." She turned and looked at me as she leaned back against the counter crossing her arms. "But it was short term and would've gotten the message across to him last night. He would've known he'd been a douche in the past and you would've walked away without having gotten involved. This plan you have going now? *Totally* messed up!"

I pushed my Pop-Tarts away having lost my appetite.

"I mean, think about it, Simone." She huffed out a humorless laugh and shook her head. "You think you can go to his house, get all cozy with him maybe even do the deed, then walk out of there like nothing happened? Never see him again? This is Hallervan we're talking about not UDub where you might get away with that. Are you freaking delusional?"

"Crap! You're right," I replied, my brain finally fricking clearing. "What was I thinking?" I stood up quickly, grabbing up my breakfast and going to the trashcan to toss it out. And, oh, joy, here came the panic. "I can't go out with him tonight or… or ever!" Now I started pacing. "What did I think would happen? We'd fuck then just move on? I couldn't do that because I'm a one-night-stand rookie! I couldn't handle not talking to him again! Or just seeing him on campus! Or anywhere! And even if I tried having a one-night stand with… with… with… *anyone*, I know I'd bomb at it because the two guys I've been with, I swear I became emotionally attached to them, like, the moment their dick was inside me! I'd be a mess if I tried walking away from Loch because I wasn't nearly as attracted to the other two like I am to him! Shit! Shit! Shit! Shit!"

When she didn't reply, I stopped pacing and looked at her and saw she was trying to hold in a laugh.

"What?" I hissed.

"I don't think I've ever heard you use so many bad words in one sentence before." She let out a snort.

"This isn't the time to be joking!" I spit out and scowled at her.

Her face sobered. "You're right. And let me just say I'm glad you finally woke up."

"I can't go tonight and I've got to tell him why." I looked at her. "I do *have* to tell him why, right?"

She chuckled. "Technically, I guess you don't have to tell him anything."

"Really?" That perked me up. Man, I really was a chickenshit.

She pushed off the counter with her bottom and walked past me, patting my arm on the way. "If you think it's over with him, you can do whatever you want."

She was right. All I had to do was call him and tell him I couldn't go tonight nor could I see him anymore. That sounded easy.

The hard part was acknowledging the fact that it was all a big lie.

Confession Number Seven

I showered and got ready for my one-to-nine shift at Game Traders, putting on black jeans then my chartreuse (yuck) t-shirt that had, in hot pink bold font, the store name above my left boob and "You abuse them, we re-use them" on the back. I put my hair in a high ponytail then pulled on my white Cons and was out the door by a quarter to one.

I'd talked to Marcy about Adam before showering, having forgotten that there was another person in the house besides myself who had a life, and found out that she was pretty much in love.

"He's great, Sim! He's so sweet and considerate. And so hot! He knows what he's doing in bed for sure. I came twice before we had actual penetration! His tongue is fucking amazing not to mention those strong fingers of his. And the size of his—"

"Okay, okay. I get it." I clapped a hand over her mouth then rolled my eyes. "Overshare," I warned as I removed my hand only to see her smirk. I mean, I guessed if I wasn't having sex at least she could indulge. I just didn't need to hear *all* the lurid details.

"Let's just say I'm definitely sore *down there* today." At my look of disgust she cracked up.

"Well, I'm happy for you and your, um, sore lady bits," I offered which made her laugh more.

"I've been thinking. Maybe you *should* tell Loch who you are. I'll bet he'd understand."

Then I told her about his *The Little Prince* tattoo.

"Oh. Maybe not. Well, I'd be willing to bet he was talking about you and not Samantha." I cut my eyes to her. "I'm serious! You weren't ugly back then. You were just… aesthetically challenged," she declared.

Now I laughed. "Ugly works too." I waved my hand at her. "Okay, enough. Stop talking about me and my severe appearance deficit. I've gotta get ready for work. I'll call him on my break and tell him we're done. Not telling him who I am. Just making a clean break of it."

"Still think you should 'fess up. I think you two sound cute together."

I mumbled something about maybe in another lifetime as I headed to the bathroom because, really, if he knew I'd played him all along he'd be pissed and I couldn't blame him. So better to nip things in the bud.

~*~*~*~

"Sim-ulator! What's up?" Thorne Verbeck called as I walked into Game Traders. He was the owner and had hired me telling me they needed a girl in the mix, whatever that meant. He had to be at least thirty but dressed like a skater dude, shaggy blond hair, saggy shorts or depending on the day, skinny jeans that sagged, Vans, and he appeared to be stoned out of his mind every time I saw him. He was tall and thin and actually kind of reminded me of Shaggy from *Scooby Doo* with his laidback attitude which was actually kind of cool. He'd been open in telling everyone he was a trust-fund baby, and from what the guys who worked there told me he'd inherited so much money that he didn't need to work for the rest of his life and had opened the store because he'd gotten bored. They said he had so much money that even his grandkids would never have to work a day in their lives. But from what I'd witnessed, he was a nice guy who donated regularly to charities that mostly had something to do with kids, giving them not only money but skateboards, having skate parks built and the like. He also paid his employees two dollars over minimum wage which was awesome.

"Hey, Thorne. Not much," I replied with a smile, going behind the counter where he sat on a stool.

"Classes going okay?"

"Yeah. I'll be the next Bill Gates before you know it."

He grinned as he nodded. "Righteous."

"Yeah, righteous," I agreed as I opened the register and did a money count.

Griffin walked to the counter. "Hey, Simone. We've sold twenty-seven games today, traded four with a discount and bought ten." He nodded at the register. "Should be even Steven in there at one twenty-five and some change."

Griffin was the assistant manager and attended UDub where he was a math major and part-time genius who, like Thorne, was high more often than not. He was short and thickly muscled and had to be in his late twenties. He had a girlfriend around the same age who came in frequently, they both had dreadlocks in their brown hair, Griffin also wore a goatee, and even though they were white, they said they were Rastafarian. They regularly wore t-shirts sporting pictures of Haile Selassie, Bob Marley, Marcus Garvey or marijuana paraphernalia as a testament to their faith, the latter "just because we can" as Griff had once explained, and since I wasn't one to judge and knew little about the religion, to each his own.

"To the penny," I responded closing the register. "You're good, Griff."

"Don't I know it," he said, holding his fist out to me to bump, which I did, but I didn't do the exploding thing after with the sound effects like he did.

"What time you get off today, Griff?" I asked.

"Off now, baby girl."

"Then you won't mind if I change the music?"

He laughed. "Go right ahead, woman. Although I'm gonna convert you to love my tunes soon."

I laughed and rolled my eyes as I headed back to the office. I highly doubted that would happen because ska or reggae or dancehall music, any of what he listened to, wasn't my thing and he knew this. I was a rock and alternative rock girl and although I did like that one 311 song he'd made me listen to that's as far as it went.

I pulled up my playlist on the laptop on Thorne's desk and right off the bat, my beloved Theory of a Deadman started singing "Angel" and all was right with my world for the time being. When I went back out to the floor I saw that both Thorne and Griffin had gone.

"I guess it's just us for now."

Crap. Dakota, who was my coworker, nineteen and the biggest horn dog I knew, was standing behind the counter checking a kid out but his eyes were on me. To date, I had to guesstimate that he'd asked me out three thousand, nine hundred and twenty-one times all of which I'd answered in the negative. Yeesh.

"Hey, Dakota," I mumbled as I headed to the shelves to sort and straighten the games. A few minutes later, he was there. Yippee.

"So, there's this party later..." I rolled my eyes as I continued working on the shelves. "And if you're not busy, I thought we could go together."

I turned to look at him. He really was a cute guy, around six-feet tall, fairly muscular, big blue eyes that had lashes out "to there" and longish brown hair that curled around his neck. But the many times he'd come in telling us about his sexual conquests had put the kibosh on my going out with him. Ever. I didn't doubt his stories because several of the girls had shown up at the store, and they were gorgeous. Or he'd come in to work with fifty hickies on his neck (hinting that they were other places on his body too) and I wasn't too keen on being a notch in the kid's bedpost. I emphasize "kid" because even though he was just over a year younger than I was, he was at that age where he was between being a goofy teenager and a man leaning more toward the goofy teenager side.

"Oh, sorry. I'm busy tonight," I remarked.

I felt bad when I saw his face fall but knew he'd find someone to take my place, he always did, so my sadness was short-lived. He started helping me straighten. "What, you got a date?"

My eyes cut to him for a second before I stated, "Yeah, I do."

"Really? With who?"

"Whom," I corrected then frowned because that was rude of me. "Just a guy," I went on.

"What's his name?"

I stopped and looked at him. "Why?"

He shrugged. "Just thought maybe I knew him."

"I doubt it. He's my age and goes to Hallervan too."

"My older sister goes there so I might know him. Maybe they went out."

I knew he was jealous and trying to make me feel the same, so point proven because there was that teenage boy side of him.

"Maybe they did. Who knows?"

When he realized he couldn't rile me, he sighed and went over to the game system that was set up at the front and displayed on a (no lie) ninety-freaking-inch TV, plopped down onto a beanbag and started playing. I smiled when a probably twelve-year-old kid who'd ridden his bike to the store went over and started playing with him. When I finished with the shelves, I went to the office and found a couple of packages, opened them, saw they were games kids had ordered then called to let them know they were in.

At six, Vegas came in. He was eighteen but acted more mature than Dakota. I'd liked him from the start. He was a smart guy and was kind of like a little brother to me, asking for advice about girls which I thought was completely awesome, and he was, of course, from Las Vegas. I'd seen on the timecards in the back that his real name was Vernon but we all felt Vegas fit him better.

"'Sup', Chun-Li?" he asked as he came in the door.

"Charlie Nash. Good to see you," I answered with a smile.

Those were the names of the characters from some video game we'd played against each other a few weeks before, each winning twice and we'd stopped after that. I honestly hadn't known what I'd been doing but I'd gained respect from him and the other guys so I was just going to let it lie and not push my "cool meter" back to zero.

"You too," he said as he came behind the counter where I sat on the stool. He was around my height, five-foot-nine, and was as muscle-bound as they come. I'd once seen him haul two kids who he'd suspected of shoplifting and who were much bigger than he was out of the store on his own. Tonight he was in his typical work wear: a Metallica t-shirt, jeans, a Pantera ball cap that he wore backwards on his shaved blond head, and white Air Force Ones. He leaned a hip against the counter. "So it worked. What you told me."

My face lit up. "Yeah?"

He nodded, smiling shyly.

He'd had a crush on a girl over the summer and had wanted to ask her out but didn't know how. He'd come to me asking how he should go about it and now he was telling me it worked. Good for him.

"Midnight movies tonight."

"Very cool. What's playing?"

"*From Here to Eternity*. Think she'll like it?"

"Oh, yeah. You will too. Lots of macho man stuff in it." I smiled.

He smiled back. "Cool."

"Okay, I'm gonna grab dinner. Shelves are sorted, money's good. Oh. Dakota's been playing all day." I glanced over at Dakota. "Against the same kid, too. Kid's parents are probably wondering where the heck he is. Good luck getting him to do anything," I said, nodding toward Dakota.

"Truck's coming at eight. Not a lot to do until then," Vegas pointed out.

"True," I agreed. "Okay, gonna run to the burger place down the road. What do you want?"

"The usual," he remarked as he read the back of a game box.

"Gotcha. Dakota?" I called.

"Yeah?"

"You want something?" I knew he'd heard us because he was nosy that way.

"Number two with onion rings and a chocolate shake!"

"Please?" I prompted.

"Please and thank you, sweetheart!" he fired back.

I rolled my eyes at Vegas who laughed because he'd been witness to Dakota's asking me out several times then I opened the register and grabbed a couple twenties. Thorne always told us he'd pay for our meals, which was okay by me. "I'll be back in a bit," I said and headed outside to get in my Jeep.

I'd decided to use this time to call Loch but as I started my vehicle, I changed my mind thinking I'd call after I got back. Yeah, that worked better.

When I returned to the store, I thought I'd wait until I was finished eating to make the call. Boy, was I the queen of chickenshit or what?

I brought the guys their food and put the change back in the register. Dakota was now sitting behind the counter with Vegas, his game partner gone, probably having been called home to eat. Since there were no customers in the store, we all ate at the counter, me standing on the outside, the guys sitting behind it.

"Sim's gotta hot date tonight," Dakota contributed between bites of his burger.

Vegas's surprised eyes met mine. "Yeah?"

I nodded then stupidly added, "Yeah, but I'm gonna call and cancel."

"Why?" Vegas asked around a bite of his bacon cheeseburger.

I bit my lip for a second but when I saw they were both staring at me waiting for an explanation, I decided to fill them in since I'd told them I was cancelling.

"Damn," Dakota muttered after I told them about Loch and the plan Marcy and I had come up with.

When Vegas stayed quiet, I looked at him to see he was staring back at me. "What?" I asked.

"Jesus, Sim. That's a long-ass time to hold a grudge," he declared.

"I know. That's why I decided to call the whole thing off," I explained yet again.

"I understand he was a prick but he was twelve."

I frowned at him. "I feel bad enough as it is, V. I don't need you rubbing it in."

"But you like this guy?" he questioned.

I looked at the ceiling and blew out a breath. "I said I do. But I've screwed everything up with him, giving him the wrong name, planning on hurting him. How can I move forward with him knowing what I was gonna do to him? It's best if I just make a clean break."

He narrowed his eyes. "Seriously? You were all up in my shit this summer telling me to ask Annica out, wouldn't lay off until I did. And now you're gonna bail because you're scared? Not cool, Sim." How the hell did he know I was scared? I was about to protest when he kept going. "See, if a girl told me what was going on, confessing she was priming me to call my shit out from something I'd done to her years before, I think I'd get that. Might be mad for a bit, but I'd respect the fact that she owned up to it. Then if she apologized, maybe told me she liked me, that's even better and my mad would probably go away. I don't know but I think you're fuckin' up."

I didn't need him clouding up my mind. "I know what I've got to do," I replied a bit angrily as my brow came down. But he was right. It wasn't just that I was scared. I was sick about what I'd planned on doing and it made me feel horrible about myself. And to be honest, I didn't want Loch to see what a horrible person I was for wanting to hurt him. So if I just walked away, he wouldn't find out which I knew was the coward's way out, but that's exactly what I was. "I'll make the call in a bit then it's done."

Dakota sat up straight at hearing that news. "Then you can go with me to the party!" When I raised an eyebrow at him, he went on. "Fuck. I've already asked Darian Conway. I guess I could call and tell her something came up." Then I practically saw the lightbulb go on over his head as he looked at me. "Or you could both go with me!" His look now turned lurid which my "get real" face challenged. "C'mon, Sim. It'd be fun."

Vegas snorted. "Only one having fun in that scenario'd be you, Dak."

"True that, bro," Dakota retorted, bumping his fist to Vegas's before realizing what was said wasn't completely a compliment. "Hey…" he mumbled with a frown.

Vegas grinned then told him, "Nah, you should probably stick with this Darian chick. I'll bet she's hot."

"Hell yeah, she is!" Dakota was off and running telling us how perky and bouncy her boobs were and how tight her ass was.

Since Vegas seemed to be enjoying the detailed description, I made my way back to the office to finish eating, leaving the guys to their pervification over poor Darian. I sat in Thorne's chair and after finishing the last of my fries, sighed. Now was as good a time as any, I thought. So wiping my hands on a napkin I then took a drink of soda before I straightened the papers on Thorne's desk. Then griping myself out for stalling, I grabbed the store's phone instead of mine to maybe catch Loch off balance because he wouldn't know it was me which would make it easier to do what I had to do. Or at least that sounded like a good plan.

I looked at my contact list on my phone and punched in his number then waited as it rang hating that I was doing this because I really liked Loch. And under any other circumstances, maybe we could've worked out but I'd gone and ruined everything by being a conniving asshole.

"Hello?" Just hearing his voice made my insides get all gooshy.

"Loch?"

"Yeah?"

"Hey, it's, uh, Celeste," I said, closing my eyes, now hating my middle name.

"Hey, babe. Was just gettin' ready to text you my address." I heard the smile in his voice and wanted to kick myself.

"That won't be necessary," I whispered.

"You already know where I live?" He sounded surprised but happy too. God!

"No."

Silence. Then, "What's going on?"

I took a deep breath and stated, "It's not going to work with us. I can't see you tonight... or any other night, Loch. I'm sorry."

I heard him whisper, "The fuck?" then I got dead air.

I hung up and closed my eyes as a single tear fell down my cheek. I wiped it away angrily knowing I didn't deserve to have any emotions when it came to Loch because I'd been nothing but a scheming witch since the first day I'd talked to him after class.

After sitting and staring at the wall for a good twenty minutes, I finally took a deep breath, telling myself I'd done the right thing and went back out onto the floor to see that the truck had come, Vegas and Dakota had put everything out and were now in front of the huge TV arguing over some video game on the screen. From what I could tell, it was a military type game and Dakota's character kept getting killed while Vegas yelled at him to listen.

Not wanting to get in the middle of it, I elected to sit behind the counter, elbows on top and chin in my hands, watching the guys and feeling sorry for myself for having lost the best thing that'd come around in a long time. After a bit, I sat up heaving out a huge sigh then looking out the windows saw that it'd started pouring rain which matched my mood perfectly. Good thing it was only fifteen minutes to closing because I needed to get home to have some serious gloom and doom time. I adjusted my position, only one elbow on the counter now and resting my head on my hand as I stared out at the dreary evening. My pouting spell went on for some time until I heard the bell on the front door jingle. I let out an annoyed huff, not wanting to deal with any customers especially teenage boys who were our usual patrons, and sitting up turned to the door then gasped so hard I almost fell off the stool.

Loch was standing there glaring at me, his amber eyes blazing with irritation, his hair dripping wet, jaw muscles jumping as drops of rain rolled down the sides of his face and off that freaking square jawline onto his soaked gray t-shirt.

As I stared back, I was torn between running to him, telling him everything and what a fool I'd been or running to the back to lock myself in the office.

Office. The office sounded good.

Just as I made my move to go, I swear, he advanced so freaking fast it was like he teleported to me because one moment I was moving from behind the counter to run down the hallway and the next, his arm was around my waist jerking me back into him making me yelp out a big "Oomph!"

It was then I knew the extent of the trouble I was in because as he held me against him, my back to his front, his head bending so that his mouth was at my ear and I heard him hiss, "Wanna tell me what the fuck's going on?" I found that I liked that he'd come for me.

Shit.

I was so screwed.

Confession Number Eight

There are moments in life that you don't want to end. You want them to last forever so you can soak it all in, commit everything to memory so that later in life you can pull these memories back up and smile.

This wasn't one of them.

I stood there speechless, my body stiff as a board and plastered to Loch's, which wasn't wholly unpleasant. And as I was deciding whether I'd like to retain that part as a memory for my later years, he jerked me against him more tightly, I guess signaling that he was waiting for an answer.

"Uh…"

His arm got tighter around my waist and I wanted to tell him that if he thought that was punishment for my not talking or his way of prompting me *to* talk, then he was so wrong. I mean, really? Let's see… turn to face him and talk or continue being held against his strong, rock hard body. Duh. Nothing tough in that decision at all, even though he was dripping water on me, but I didn't care one bit.

"Celeste…" I heard him warn and it was then I noticed that Vegas and Dakota had come up, both not looking very happy that I was being detained by someone they didn't know.

"You wanna step off, man?" Vegas snarled dangerously giving Loch a very pointed look. Dakota took a step forward his menacing look just as scary as Vegas's. Whoa. I didn't know they cared that much about me.

"It's okay, guys," I offered, finding it hard to act carefree seeing how I was encased by the muscular arm and held against the equally muscular body of a man who I'm sure was mirroring my two coworkers' intimidating looks.

Vegas's assessing eyes held mine. "You sure, Simone?"

I nodded letting him know I was fine.

"Just give me the word, Simone, and I'll drop him," Dakota added, and from the look on his and Vegas's faces, I knew they'd pounce if I gave them the go ahead.

"It's okay, guys," I said.

"Simone?" Loch asked.

And I froze. I mean, completely stopped breathing and everything.

Shit.

Shit!

I hadn't even realized they'd used my real name and now I felt Loch's body go solid behind me.

"Yeah, Simone St. John," Dakota provided, narrowing his eyes at Loch. "I'll bet you're the guy who was fuckin' rude to her at that dance when you were young, aren't you? Well, she and her roommate Marcy decided to get you back for it. Fool you into thinking she was someone else then she'd slam the door right in your face. And guess what, man? You fell for it. Are you a dumbass or what?" He snorted.

I stared at Dakota shocked that he'd just laid it all out there. Loch's arm dropped from around my waist and I felt him step away from me. All I could do was stand frozen, still staring at my coworkers because no way could I turn and look Loch in the face now. As I kept my eyes on Vegas and Dakota I saw they were both watching him then I frowned when both their eyes cut to the door which was when I heard it open.

Then spinning around, I watched as Loch walked out into the rain with not even a glance back.

Shit!

A moment of indecision blasted through me as I stood there biting my lip. I wanted to go after him and tell him what an idiot I was, how stupid I was to even think of hurting him.

But in the end, I decided it was for the best to let him go.

And I paid majorly for that decision. My chest got tight and it felt like I was sipping my air in through a straw. Then my vision closed to a pinpoint, the black creeping in, and reaching for something to steady myself before I passed out, I felt someone take my hand then a strong arm went around my waist and I was being led to the barstool.

Vegas.

"You all right?" he asked as he helped me sit.

It took me a moment to focus then I saw his worried face as he bent down in front of me. I nodded weakly, my breaths still raspy, then I heard him tell Dakota to get me some water. Momentarily, Dakota came back with a bottle of water, opened it and handed it to me.

After taking a few sips I got my wits about me and mumbled, "Thanks," as the backs of my eyes stung.

"You good?" Dakota asked, eyebrows raised.

"Yeah," I answered in the affirmative as I shook my head in the negative. It wasn't hard to see that even though my mind was in one place, my body, my heart, was in another.

"It's gonna be okay. It's all taken care of now," Vegas remarked with a frown.

I looked at Dakota. "I was gonna try to be a bit nicer about it," my voice cracked, "but I think you pretty much took care of things."

"Just told it like it was. Dude deserved it for being a prick to you," Dakota clarified.

I sucked in a shaky breath as I nodded. "Well, I'm sure he hates me now."

Vegas rubbed my back. "You knew the whole thing was pretty shitty," he said quietly.

"I know," I agreed.

"Just gotta pick up the pieces now," Vegas suggested.

My shoulders dropped and I hung my head as the tears began to fall. "I'm so stupid."

"You're not stupid, Sim. Look, you've helped me a lot with Annica." He ducked his head trying to get me to look at him. "Now it's my turn to help you."

I finally looked up to see he'd taken his hat off and was scrubbing his hand over his shortly cropped hair before returning the cap. He'd done that a lot when he asked for advice on the girl, Annica, who he wanted to ask out and I knew it meant he was uncomfortable with my crying. Dakota was nowhere to be found.

I let out a deep sigh as I brushed the tears from my face. "How can you help me, V? Were you telling the truth earlier? That if a girl did this to you, you'd really wanna talk to her again?"

"Depends on if she's hot or not. If so, yeah, but probably not right away. If not, hell no! I'm handing the bitch her walking papers!" Dakota popped back in from where he'd gone to get away from the pathetic crying girl.

"Shut the fuck up, man," Vegas snapped at him. "If the girl's puttin' out, you know you'd forgive her either way." Vegas looked at me. "Were you puttin' out?"

Good grief.

"No!" This made me start crying again for some reason and again Dakota disappeared.

Vegas held his hands up to his sides. "Okay, sorry. Look, here's the deal. You basically lied to him, right? I guess it all comes down to how much he hates being lied to." He shrugged.

This made me cry harder. "Then I'm screwed." Screwed came out more as "screw-ooh-ooh-ooh-ed." I explained, "When we went to the Pool Party..." now I was really boohooing, "I went to call Marcy and tell her I wasn't going to hurt him. When I came back, he was talking to a girl. Then he told her he was done with her!" I was sobbing now. "He told her... he told her to leave him the fuck alone!" I saw Dakota come up and disappear again. Vegas handed me some tissue that I guess Dakota had retrieved from the restroom. "He said she'd tried to be someone she wasn't when she was with him. He considered that lying and basically said he hated liars." I wiped at my tears then started doing that stupid hiccup-y crying thing where you try talking but it's like you can only get one syllable out at a time. "So... bas... i... cal... ly... we're... done."

"He's got to care, Sim. I mean, he *did* come all the way over here just to see what was going on," Vegas declared.

I could've hugged him for being so sweet to me. "Y-you... th... ink?"

He nodded.

I thought on this for a moment and since I was pretty much finished bawling, Dakota reappeared. "That's true," he agreed. "If it were me and I got a call or text from the girl explaining everything, that'd help a lot."

I perked up a bit because that sounded hopeful. "R-really?"

Vegas nodded before he grinned. "But then I'd expect her to put out."

"Hell yeah." Dakota nodded also grinning.

I had to chuckle at my horny friends as I ran the tissue under my eyes.

"Text him then call him," Vegas repeated. I wrinkled my brow and he said it again. "Do it."

"Yeah. Couldn't hurt," Dakota added.

I nodded, finally pulling myself together. "Okay. I'll call him. Thanks, guys."

"You need more guy advice, you know where to find us," Dakota answered then went to shut down the video game they'd been playing and turn off the TV.

"You've got this, Sim," Vegas, who'd stayed behind encouraged.

"Thanks, V," I said as I stood then pulled him in for a hug. "You're the best," I told him when I stepped back.

He smiled almost shyly then went to grab the carpet sweeper to make a few passes over the area where traffic was heaviest. I got the money bag out of the drawer under the register and filled it with the day's proceeds. When Vegas came back behind the counter to put the sweeper away, I had to know. "What if he won't talk to me? What if he really does hate me?"

He lifted a shoulder. "Won't know until you try," he answered then went to lock the front doors.

I nodded hating the mess I was in then walked back to the office to lock the money in the safe. The guys met me in the hallway and we all walked out the back door. As I pulled the key out of the lock, I felt a hand on my shoulder. Turning, I saw Dakota's patronizing face right there.

"I know you've had a bad night, Sim, but this should cheer you up. My offer's still on the table for you to go to the party with me. I know Darian will understand and we might even be able to hook you up with someone cool. If not, you're more than welcome to hang with us."

I let out a sobby laugh and scrunched my nose up. "Uh, thanks, Dakota, but I'll pass."

"You got my number if you change your mind."

We walked to our cars, Dakota to his 2001 Taurus, which always made me smile to see someone with such a cocky attitude driving such a tame car, and Vegas to his 1970 Torino which definitely fit his personality, all muscle car badass.

I got into my Jeep but before I closed my door, Vegas hollered, "It's gonna be fine, Sim. Have faith." I turned to see him giving me a thumbs up and gave him a small smile back wishing I could be as confident as he was.

~*~*~*~

On my way home, Marcy texted letting me know she was staying with Adam which was fine by me because I found I was mad at her for ever suggesting Triple C and I probably would've said something not very nice to her. Even though I knew my situation wasn't all her fault, she'd been the one to egg it on so we needed to have a talk soon to straighten things out.

As I pulled up into the drive, I decided to call my brother since I hadn't talked to him in a couple weeks. I also needed to hear a friendly voice with all the turmoil that was my life at the moment.

"What's up, baby sis?" he answered which made me smile.

"Hey, Tris. Just getting home from work. What's going on?" I unlocked the front door of the rent house and went inside.

"Nada. Sky and I are just chillin' by the pool, havin' some frou frou shit she's making me drink."

I heard Sky giggle and knew she'd smacked him when Tris laughed and said, "Ouch!"

They were so cute together and I'd always wanted a relationship like theirs. But I'd be willing to bet that Sky hadn't pulled the crap on Tris like I had on Loch.

"Sounds fun," I mumbled as I plopped down on the couch.

"What's wrong?"

I took a breath and let it out. "Guy problems."

"Lemme let you talk to Sky."

I laughed at how quickly he passed the phone to his girlfriend.

"Hey, Sim, what's going on, sweetie?" Sky asked in her very cool raspy voice that reminded me of Polly Draper's or Cathy Moriarty's. I'd always envied what Mom called Sky's whiskey voice because she sounded awesome when she talked.

"Hey, Sky. It's kind of a long story."

"I've got time. Your brother's getting smashed on girly drinks anyway."

I heard her snort as Tris retorted, "I'm all man, baby! Gimme Lagavulin any day to this shit!"

"I know you are, baby. And I love that about you. But let me talk to Simone right now, okay? So what's the deal?" she asked.

I told her everything from beginning to end. She'd known a little about how I'd retreated into myself when I was younger, she just didn't know the cause of it.

"Oh, honey, that makes perfect sense now. I'm so sorry that happened to you. And I don't think you're horrible for what you did. I don't think Marcy is either. She loves you and had been hurt too and wanted a little retribution is all. She just went about it the wrong way. I'm sure she feels bad for putting you in the middle."

"Thanks, Sky."

"And I'd say definitely call him. Don't text because they're hard to get connotations sometimes, you know? But, sweetie, be prepared if he's not too receptive to an apology. But I'll bet he'll come around eventually. I'm sure he feels betrayed, maybe even foolish for not recognizing you and we both know how sensitive a man's ego is," she stated.

"Hey, now," I heard Tris say in the background.

"It's true, baby," Sky declared before coming back to me. "Anyway, yes, call him and find out where his head is then you'll be able to stop fretting."

"Okay. Thanks. Hey, put me on speaker for a sec, okay?"

"Hold on." Then she informed me, "You're on!"

"I love you guys. We need to go to dinner soon, okay?" I heard their responses of agreement to have dinner and that they both loved me which made me feel a bit better. "Bye!"

After hanging up, I sat on the sofa contemplating what Sky had told me hoping she was right that Loch would eventually come around. I decided I'd call him in thirty minutes, thinking he probably wouldn't pick up anyway and actually kind of hoping he wouldn't. To kill time, I watched a bit of TV then when it was ten-thirty, I went to get ready for bed thinking I'd make the call from there.

I changed into my pjs, flossed, then brushed my teeth… then went to the kitchen and ate a brownie from the batch I'd made that morning… went back to the bathroom and flossed and brushed again, then felt I should shower which I did… then put on a different pair of pjs… went back to the kitchen and grabbed a diet soda to neutralize the calories from the brownie, drank it, went again to the bathroom to floss and brush… and then I was ready to make the call.

I sat cross-legged on my bed and stared at my phone for a while before picking it up. Then I put it back down. Then I picked it up, brushed my thumb over it, flopped back on the bed, pulled up Candy Crush and played a few times. When I closed the game and saw that it was after eleven, realizing I'd wasted a good hour and a half from when I'd hung up with Tris and Sky, I knew it was time to be a big girl and make the call.

Taking a deep breath, I pulled up his number and called. Then I immediately hung up and threw the phone on my bed again.

"Eff! Eff, eff, eff, eff! I'm such a jackwagon! Suck it up and just call him already! God!" I scolded myself. I picked up the phone and was about to try again when I saw I hadn't properly hung up and the call was engaged.

And I think I saw Jesus right at that very frickin' moment.

Holy fracking frack!

I stared at my phone in mortal shock and wheezed as I tried sucking in a breath. Then bringing the phone to my ear, I whispered, "Hello?"

"Yo."

"Um, Loch?" I kept whispering.

"Ryker."

Oh, holy yikes!

I felt all the color drain from my face before saying, "Oh. Hi, Ryker. It's, um, Simone St. John." I was going for casual.

I don't think I achieved it.

"Huh. Thought that was you last night. Can't believe Loch didn't figure that shit out."

At least Ryker hadn't told on me which was one good thing. Well, would you look at me finding the silver lining and all! Ergh.

"Um, yeah. I'm sure you know what I was planning… uh, not telling him who I was then leading him on only to tell him to take a hike because he'd been mean to me when we were young." Hearing it all laid out like that just made it sound so lame now.

"Yep. I figured as much. Hey, did I just hear you say 'jackwagon'?" I heard him snort which kind of ticked me off because the last thing I needed was him making fun of me. And seriously, all of this just needed to be over with. Now.

"Yeah, I guess you did," I replied a bit testily. Then gathering all the courage I had and facing my fears I forged ahead. "So… is Loch there?"

Ryker chuckled. "Yeah. He's here."

I waited for him to give Loch the phone. Then I waited some more. Then a bit more.

Well. Ryker was either not a very smart man or he was a man who was going to make me say what I wanted. When he still stayed silent, I knew it was the latter. Jeez.

"Can I talk to him?" I said semi-exasperatedly.

He chuckled again. "He's kinda indisposed right now."

What the heck did that mean?

Then I heard a girl giggling in the background before she let out a squeal of, "Loch! Stop!"

Ha. Indisposed indeed. I felt my entire body get tight as my breathing got shallower. I was *such* an idiot to put myself through this thinking I even mattered to him.

"Oh. Well, okay, I'll, uh, let you go then."

"Simone?"

"Yeah?" I choked out.

"You give it some time, maybe call him when he's not so fucked up on Jack Daniels he can't fuckin' see straight, he might be willin' to work shit out," Ryker shared.

"He's drunk?"

"Came home, soakin' wet and pissed as hell, grabbed the bottle from the cabinet not botherin' with a glass then downed half the fucker right there, wet clothes and all. Asked him what was up, all he said was, 'Simone St. John.' Knew things had turned sour then."

Ya think? I didn't dare say that to Ryker, though. He was scary enough as it was. Just having this conversation with him was scary in itself. He'd never talked much when he was little and the fact that he was telling me all this was just weird.

"But he's got a woman over there now," I whispered, pointing out the obvious.

"Nah. That's just Nikki. She's a, uh, friend of mine."

Oh, I'm sure Ryker, as hot as he was, had lots of "friends" but I didn't say anything because I was listening to Loch and Nikki in the background arguing over what I guessed was a video game, my limited knowledge from Game Traders coming into play for once.

"Tell you what," Ryker began. "You text him tomorrow, early. He answers or not, call him tomorrow night, I guarantee he'll be up to listen."

"Why're you being so nice to me after what I did?" I blurted then cringed.

He barked out a laugh. "First of all, you caught me when I'm pretty fuckin' fried myself. Second, my little brother doesn't give his time to just anyone. Obviously, you mean somethin' to him or he wouldn't be drinkin' away his sorrows right now. Third, you owned up to shit by callin' which shows me you got character and just might be worth his time." He paused for a beat as I sat stunned at what he'd said. "And I know how you felt about him when we were kids. He told me what he did at that dance, felt bad he did that to you. Just took the 'jackwagon,'" he snorted at his use of my ridiculous word, "some time to figure that shit out. By the time he did, you were gone. You'da played shit straight up this time, you'd be here right now instead o' sittin' at home lickin' your wounds."

Well. Ryker did not mess around with his words.

But he was so right and I was a dumbass. "Thank you, Ryker," I said, seriously grateful he'd picked up the phone.

"No problem, babe." I heard Nikki let out a loud giggle then Loch shouted, "Fuck yeah!" and Ryker spit out a, "Fuck!" Then I heard him blow out a breath. "Gotta go. They've busted out the tequila. Shit just got fuckin' real. Might wanna wait on that text 'til tomorrow night."

"Okay. Thanks again," I replied but he'd already hung up.

Great. Here I was sitting at home all alone when I could've right then been at Loch's watching badass blow-'em-up macho man flicks, probably making out hardcore with him before, during and after each movie. Instead, he was getting plastered with some woman who was almost certainly a friend-with-benefits of Ryker's, and I cringed when I wondered if Loch had a couple of them too who he might very well invite over.

I got up off my bed, pulled back my covers then slipped in between them. Then I lay there staring at my ceiling for who knows how long going over different scenarios in my head (which was a total waste of time but whatever) of how I should've handled things in class last Wednesday. When I got tired of beating myself up over the real-life scenario I'd actually chosen, I reached over and turned off my light.

I got into my going to sleep position but knew I wouldn't be falling asleep anytime too soon. I also knew I had no one to blame for how things had turned out but myself.

And that sucked.

A lot.

Confession Number Nine

What seemed like only seconds after I drifted off, my eyes popped open and my breath was coming hard at the nightmare I'd just had. I felt the tears welling up in my eyes and I sat up leaning my back against the wall at the head of my bed as I allowed the tears to fall for a few minutes because the dream had been beyond disturbing. When I stopped crying, I went to the kitchen to get a drink.

As I stood with my butt against the counter, still sniffing from my tears, I wondered how in the heck my mind had even allowed itself to even go there.

In the dream, I'd gotten out of bed and dressed then gone to Loch's (even though in reality I had no idea where he lived). I'd pulled up to a nice house and saw his truck parked in the drive along with several other vehicles. When I got out of my Jeep, I heard music blasting from the house and walking toward it saw the front door was open so I went inside. I was then in a dark living room that had a TV with a video game playing on it but the sound was muted. A light was coming from the hallway so I went toward it calling for Loch over the loud music. Down the hall I saw the light was coming from a room, so going to it, I pushed it open, belatedly realizing "Closer" by Nine Inch Nails was the song playing, and looking inside, just like the lyrics of the song, saw Loch having wild animal sex with the pretty blond girl he'd argued with at the Pool Party. At my gasp, he turned his head and smiled cruelly at me as he kept screwing her, his hips thrusting hard into her as she looked at me and laughed. I turned away for a moment, planning to get the hell out of there, but when I looked back at the girl I saw she'd turned into Marcy and that's when I'd woken up.

Holy fuck.

Fuck.

Fuck.

Fuck!

Definitely a cussword moment.

I finished my water then set the glass in the sink and scrubbed my hand over my face, shuddering at the memory of the nightmare and thinking Marcy would have a field day with it. But standing there, arms now crossed and rubbing my hands up and down my biceps, I'd never felt so alone in my life. Even when I'd withdrawn in middle school, I knew my family had been there. But right then, right in that very moment, it seemed as if it was just me against the world. And I hated that feeling.

I let out a sigh then walked back to my room finished with all the depressing crap. After getting in bed I looked at my phone to see it was only a quarter after midnight which meant I'd only been asleep for about ten minutes when I'd awakened from the stupid nightmare. My mind must've been in an awesome place to come up with what it had.

I stared at the ceiling for a bit then turned on my side, squeezing my eyes closed trying to force myself to sleep, so ready to get this night over with. And lo and behold, sleep came, beautiful, gorgeous, dreamless sleep which was then interrupted an hour later by my phone buzzing on my nightstand and lighting up my room like the bastard beacon it was.

"You've got to be kidding me," I murmured, reaching over to grab it. "What?" I ground out upon answering it.

"Suh-leste," Loch said drunkenly.

Oh shit.

I sat up quickly, scrunching up my face and putting my hand to my forehead feeling horrible (yet again) about how everything had gone down.

"Loch," I whispered waiting for him to castigate me in his crocked condition.

"Y'lied."

Yep. I'd lied. "I know and I'm sorry."

"Why'dja do it?"

I swallowed thickly. "Because I was an idiot. I'm so sorry, Loch."

"Should be you here… not her…"

And my heart flew to my throat. I closed my eyes wondering if I was psychic and my dream had just been a foretelling of what was really happening.

Damn it.

Damn it!

"Who's there?" I asked, not really wanting to know the answer.

"Should b'you…"

"Loch, hang up," I heard a woman grouchily demand.

God!

"Should b'you, Suh-leste… or S'mone… whatever the fuck your name is." He was getting mad now but so was I.

"Yeah, get off the phone, Loch," I snapped and hung up.

Well, that was that.

I tossed my phone back on the nightstand and lay back down feeling even worse than I had after the nightmare. I knew guys our age. Knew how they operated. I'd seen it time and again with the ones I or my friends had dated. You got in a fight. They left mad. They got drunk. They slept with someone else. Then they wanted to make amends with you.

It was one big vicious circle of immature retaliation, and I never understood why they'd think a girl would come back to them after they did that.

So again, that was that.

But I'd thought Loch was different but why should he be? He was a guy of that age. It only made sense. So even though I'd thought I'd been done with him when I returned to Seattle, I was done-r than done now.

And to prove it, I locked my heart up tight… then cried myself to sleep.

~*~*~*~

"We need to talk," I informed Marcy the next morning.

It was after ten when I walked into the kitchen to find her toasting waffles. At my saying this and at her seeing my face, I watched as her usually sleepy, grumpy self woke up quickly.

"About?" she asked, eyebrows up.

"I'm a bad person."

She chuckled then quickly pulled the waffles out of the toaster when it popped up and tossed them on a plate.

"Why's that?" she inquired as she walked to the table. She then sat down, picked up the bottle of syrup and proceeded to pour almost half of it onto her plate.

I got a glass out and poured some orange juice in it, turning to look at her. "I kinda blamed you for everything with Loch."

Her eyebrows went up again but it didn't keep her from shoving a forkful into her mouth. I went to the table and sat then told her all that'd happened the night before including the dream.

"That's a lot happening in one night," she said.

I nodded because she was not wrong.

"I'm sorry, Sim. You *should* blame me. I guess I kinda used you, didn't I? To get back at Loch. I never should've suggested you do that." My eyebrows went up now. "Okay, talked you into doing it. That was shitty advice and I'm to blame for the mess you're in."

I frowned. "Wasn't like I didn't agree to do it. It's not all your fault, Marce."

"Yeah, but I put it in your head. Sorry. You forgive me?"

I gave her a small smile, nodded then took a drink.

"You know I wanna tell you what the dream meant," she prompted.

I snorted because I knew she was itching to tell me. "Yep. But maybe as punishment, I won't let you."

"That's just fucked up."

I laughed. "Maybe. But you *are* getting off scot free here."

"Never. Your pain is my pain, babe."

And that's why I loved her and forgave her so willingly. I gave her a smile and returned, "Back at you."

"So as for the dream…" she started and I chuckled knowing she couldn't let it lie. "Well, I'm sure you've figured it out. Your insecurities mixed with your anger at me brought it on."

I nodded.

"So what're you gonna do about things with him?"

"Really isn't much to do." I shrugged.

"You could talk to him."

"No. I don't think that's necessary. Here's the deal. If he'd just been some guy I met and we'd had an argument then he called me drunk and I knew he had a girl over, I'd be over it." I shrugged. "I knew I was more invested with Loch because of our past but why can't I be over it now too? Yeah, it hurt me. Yeah, I screwed up. But why do I have to brood over it? I liked him. I made out with him a couple times. But I've only just *now* known him for what, five days? I'll get over it."

"You sure?"

"Yeah. And all I just said is true. I don't know why I let everything from the past seem so devastating to me up until now. I guess because I was an insecure little girl. But now that I followed your 'shitty' advice," I grinned at her as she gave me a funny face, "I tried doing something mean to him as payback, which made me come off as a bitch, and I got burned. Game over."

"Oooh, work talk," she declared with a chuckle.

I chuckled too. "Anyway, there's no future for Loch and me. All I can do now is try to be his friend. Be nice to him. If he doesn't want that, then I'm good."

And I was. I hoped.

I finished my juice and got up from the table. "Gotta get ready for work. You and Adam doing okay?" I asked over my shoulder as I rinsed my glass out then put it and the one from last night in the dishwasher.

She smiled. "More than okay. I think I'm falling for him."

This made me smile. "Good for you." I stood straight and turned to her as I closed the dishwasher door. "You deserve to be in love."

"You do too, Sim."

I cocked my head letting her know I wasn't ready to go there any time too soon after the debacle with Loch.

"You do. And honestly, if you really do like Loch, I think you should go for it."

I shook my head. "Not happening." I walked past her to go to my room and get dressed.

"Just follow your heart!" she called after me.

I huffed out a humorless laugh at that. After what had gone down, I'd put my heart on moratorium for now and I wasn't too fired up to end it.

So as far as I was concerned, Loch Powers would just have to be a lesson learned.

~*~*~*~

My shift at Game Traders was from noon to six which was when the store closed on Sundays. I knew neither Thorne nor Griffin would be in because they'd told us once that "Saturday nights are for bonging out" and they needed Sunday to recuperate. I hadn't looked at the schedule last night before I left, so I wasn't sure who I'd be working with today.

"Don't be Dakota, don't be Dakota," I whispered as I signaled to turn off the street into the store's parking lot. I just wasn't in the mood to hear about how he'd nailed Darian last night or any other disgusting crap he'd try sharing. Pulling into the lot behind the store, I let out a sigh of relief when I saw that Vegas was waiting at the back door and smoking a cigarette.

"Those'll stunt your growth," I scolded as I dug my keys out of my purse as I walked toward him.

"Haven't had any complaints," he muttered connotatively taking a last drag before flicking the cigarette away.

Of course he made it sexual and I didn't have any smartassed comeback so I remained silent. But now I realized I was in a bad mood from thinking on my drive over about just being friends with Loch, knowing I didn't want to just be friends with him. I wanted to *be* with him. I unlocked the door and went inside, flipping on the lights as I did while Vegas followed.

"You okay?" he asked, leaning against the jamb of the office door and throwing me a concerned look.

"Fine," I mumbled, unlocking the office.

"Fuck," I heard him say as I went inside to open the safe.

I turned to look at him, lifting an eyebrow, crossing my arms and cocking one hip out in my I'm-not-putting-up-with-any-crap-today pose. "What?"

His posture mirrored mine. Well, instead of his hip, he cocked his head to the side but also crossed his arms over his chest. "When a woman says, 'Fine,' that means the total fuckin' opposite of fine. That means a shitstorm's brewing and heads are fixin' to roll."

I glared at him. "'Fixin' to'?"

He shook his head and I saw one side of his mouth tip up. "Point proven."

My glare turned to a glower. "Men are assholes." I knelt down to open the safe, pulling the money bag out then stood and passed by him not bothering to give him another look.

"I'm gatherin' things didn't go well with your man last night." He'd followed me to the counter.

As I opened the register, I ground out, "He's not my man."

"So what happened?"

I stopped putting the money in and gave him a look. "Swear to God, Vegas, I love you, but you need to stop talking before I pull a Ronda Rousey on your ass."

He started laughing and when he didn't stop I turned to stare icily at him. This only made him laugh harder.

"Jerk," I muttered as I walked by him, bumping my shoulder into him threateningly which now made him howl with laughter. I stomped to the front door to unlock it then to the shelves to do some straightening, but since I'd just straightened them the night before, there wasn't much to do. I went back to the counter thinking maybe I could rearrange the display inside.

"Come play some *Mario Kart* with me," Vegas hollered from the front. "I'll even let you win a game."

Now, *Mario Kart* I could do and he knew this. He also knew by goading me with trash talking he could entice me to play.

So of course, I fell for it. "*Let* me win? Please." I joined him, flopping down into one of the huge beanbags beside him and he handed me a controller.

We played for almost six hours straight, smack talking each other the whole time, naturally stopping when customers came in, and to be honest, it was the best therapy ever because I found myself rarely thinking about the mess I'd made. Kudos to Mario!

When it was six, we shut everything down and headed out.

"Still tied," Vegas said as we went out the back.

"Yep." I locked the back door then retorted, "Only because you *let* me win." That was a lie and he knew it. I could hold my own with that game for sure and probably could've taken him, but again we'd decided to keep it even.

He chuckled as we walked to our cars. "Nah. It's because *you* let *me* win."

"I was feeling pretty magnanimous today," I replied with a snort.

"'Least you're in a better mood now."

I had a hand on my Jeep's door when I felt my shoulders fall because what he said only served to remind me that my life was a total dung-hole right now.

"Fuck," he echoed his comment from when we'd first gotten to work. "Sorry, Sim. Goddamn it."

I looked at him then stood up straight. "You know what, V? It's okay. I'm tired of being a mopey drama queen. I'm over it." I smiled at him to prove it. Mom had always said, "Fake it 'til you make it" and I was going to put that advice to use, so sick of being a sad sack. "And I'm swearing off men at least until this semester is over."

He eyed me for a second waiting for me to break, I guess, but when I didn't, he smiled back. "Thatta girl. 'Kay, see you, what, Wednesday?"

"Yep. Be good."

"Tall order," he mumbled before he got in his Torino and fired it up. Jesus, that thing was loud.

He waited until I pulled out and gave him a wave before he put it in gear, following me out of the lot. Then I turned right and he turned left and that was that.

Confession Number Ten

Monday morning I was up and out the door before Marcy even got out of the shower. I'd decided that all the sulking I'd been doing was ridiculous, I was done with it and I was ready for the new day.

I'd called Mom when I got home from work last night and she set me back on track after I had a long talk with her about everything. She'd admonished me for keeping what'd happened at the sixth grade dance from her and Dad, but otherwise, she'd supported me in everything else I told her.

"You have to believe in yourself, Simone, before anyone else will," she'd told me. And when I'd told her about Marcy and my pitiful plan to hurt Loch like he'd hurt me, she'd advised, *"La vengeance est un plat qui se mange froid."*

Revenge is a dish best served cold.

Then she'd explained, "Most people think that means to wait until you're no longer upset so you can think clearly on how to get proper revenge on someone, while others think it means to wait until the person least expects it. But the way I interpret it is that if you wait, you'll come to realize that seeking revenge just isn't worth it."

And I so loved her for not saying right after that, "So was it worth it?"

But, man, was she ever right. It was definitely not worth it. At all.

After we'd said our I love yous and hung up, I'd actually gotten a good night's sleep for a change.

Thank you, Mom. Gosh, just talking to her had helped me put things into perspective and get my head on right and I felt a kabillion times better about everything.

So here it was Monday morning and I felt like myself again, not bogged down in all the yuckiness I'd been feeling after running into Loch. Who would've thought so much could happen in just one weekend. Jeez. But even though my confidence had made a comeback, as I got closer to campus, I panicked just a bit knowing I'd see him in class and I wasn't sure how it would go. I didn't think he'd cause a scene but I didn't know him well enough to make that call.

I went inside Noble Hall and walked to my classroom keeping my eyes down and making sure not to look around so I'd avoid the risk of seeing him. Inside the classroom, I walked straight to the same seat I'd sat in last week and finally had to laugh at myself for how serious I'd been taking myself in trying to avoid Loch. Jesus. I was behaving like a Russian spy in some political thriller. Next thing you know, I'd be doing somersaults then plastering myself to the walls as I made my way around campus.

I was still chuckling when I put my bag down and noticed that Cute Guy's girlfriend had traded places with him so he wouldn't be sitting by me anymore. The snitty look she gave me when I sat down made me bite my lips to keep the cackle I wanted to blast at her in.

I wished I could tell her there was no way in hell I was a threat since I was finished with guys for a while, but she looked like she needed to eat a cheeseburger and I didn't want to deal with a grumpy undereater chewing me out, so I let it go. Anyway, Dr. Lykins came in just then and jumped right into inductive proofs, and let the note-taking begin.

Things were good. I maintained focus on the lecture and my notes until midway through class when Dr. Lykins stopped to mess with his laptop to pull up an illustration on the Smart Board. And there was that feeling like I was being watched. I resisted for as long as I could, probably a good twenty seconds (yeah, I know, whoop-ti-do), before I looked to my left to see Loch smirking at me. When my eyes got big, his smirk did the same, and I turned to face the front again.

Hm. Maybe he wasn't mad after all. He was smirking which was kind of a smile, right? I ventured another glance at him to see him talking to the girl next to him who was giggling at something he was saying. He was talking animatedly, using his hands and I narrowed my eyes, wondering what he was talking about.

Then he looked back at me and so did the girl (EEP!) and I didn't know what his expression was saying. He wasn't smiling but he also wasn't frowning. It didn't look like indifference, thank God, but I couldn't put a finger on it. The girl was letting it all hang out though, squinting at me, examining me like I was an insect under a magnifying glass and she didn't look happy.

Great. We were back to sixth grade again. He'd told her what I'd done and was spreading it around. Nice.

I looked away just as Dr. Lykins got the board working, so picking up my pencil I flipped the page in my notebook to begin the task of transcribing his words once again, still feeling eyes on me. Still wondering what had been said. But I let it go and got lost in the world of loop invariants.

When we were dismissed, I packed up my things then made my way to the door. Out of the corner of my eye, I saw that Loch was still standing at his table talking to a guy so I hurried out. He and I had the next two classes together so maybe if I got inside quickly I could get somewhere I didn't have to look at him.

As I walked across campus, I noticed that the trees were particularly beautiful right now, their leaves just starting to turn the lovely colors of fall. In a month they'd be breathtaking with their gorgeous displays of color. I really loved Hallervan's campus with its abundance of Japanese maples whose leaves would soon be stunning. The landscaping all across the quad was lovely with the multitude of flowerbeds filled with poppies, asters and dahlias. I was enjoying my walk until I heard two guys talking behind me.

"She's fuckin' hot, dude. I don't care if she's a bitch, you need to tap that immediately," one guy said.

"She's definitely a bitch but look at that ass, man, all heart-shaped and just begging for me to sink my teeth into it," the other guy replied.

Shit. Loch was behind me and I was pretty sure he was talking about me.

I clenched my fists and spun around to give him a big fat piece of my mind and just as I opened my mouth to spew a salvo of such vitriol at him he wouldn't know what hit him, I saw two guys I didn't know looking at the phone one of them was holding up as they walked.

Oh.

They passed by me with nary a glance as one guy told the other he needed to "get in there and bang the shit out of her."

I huffed out a (kind of disgusted) laugh, rolling my eyes as I did, but the amusing moment didn't last because behind them, I saw walking right toward me with what I can only describe as a fierce-as-hell look, was Loch, the perma-smirk in full force as he looked my way.

Crap.

I spun on my heel and walked quickly to my next class wanting to cover my ears as I heard his amused chuckle. Jeez.

I made it to class and managed to avoid looking at him even when he now walked in with two pretty blondes who were fawning all over him. I could hear what they were saying to him through hushed giggles and I think part of my breakfast came up.

"Loch, you're so muscular! You would totally be the star of any sport you played here!" Thing One said.

"Oh, my gawd! You look just like that Canadian model actor guy! I thought he was hot but you're *so* much hotter!" That would be Thing Two putting in her two cents.

Seriously? Was this really happening? It was like Loch was living in a real-live 1950s beach blanket movie.

And not to be a snob, well, yeah, I was definitely being a snob, but surely these girls weren't computer majors. My eyes went to the ceiling as I waited for the professor to come in and end the madness.

I waited until Loch and his entourage left when class ended before I followed, staying at least twenty yards behind but had to stop when one of the Doublemint Twins stopped and turned a pouty face to Loch. I watched as he knelt down in front of her, took off her stiletto, checked her foot then slipped the shoe back on grinning up at her. Well, wasn't he the gentleman? I rolled my eyes when she said something about being just like Cinderella. Ergh.

Walking into my next class I saw the Bobbsey Twins sitting on either side of Loch in the front row. Studiously keeping my eyes off them, I went and sat, again managing not to glance their way. Well, that is until in the middle of class, one of the girls raised her hand.

"Um, Professor Stowe? I moved from the dorm to an apartment yesterday. I haven't turned on my laptop yet. Will all my programs still be on it even if it's not using the campus's wifi now?"

Holy smokes.

Definitely not a computer major. I listened as everyone chuckled as Dr. Stowe assured her the programs would be there.

Huh.

When class was finally over I gave a sigh, glad I no longer had to avert my eyes away from Loch and the Sweet Valley Twins. They'd already left anyway, so gathering my things I left the classroom and walked down the hall and out the front doors of South Hall. As I started toward the stairs, I came up short when I saw Loch (minus his admirers), leaning a shoulder against one of the big columns in front, backpack at his feet, arms and ankles crossed and eyes narrowed on me.

He really was handsome and *did* resemble that model guy, maybe even looked better.

Too bad I'd screwed it all up between us because I'd really liked him.

Anyway, since he was alone, I thought now would be the perfect time for me to apologize, lay it all out there and let him know that what I had planned to do to him was horrible. So mustering every ounce of courage I had, I walked his way seeing that his golden eyes stayed locked on me, so intense and dark and I swear my blood pressure shot up to *What the hell are you doing?* over *Are You Trying to Get Us Killed?*

When I got within ten feet of him and just as I opened my mouth to tell him I was sorry, a guy came out of the building and hollered, "Yo, Loch! Thanks for waiting, bro."

I turned in an arc, tilting my head to the side and veering away from him toward the steps as if that was my intention the entire time, clutching my bag to my chest and trying to keep my heart from flopping out right there onto the sidewalk. Then I hightailed it the heck out of there and kept walking fast toward the parking lot on the other side of campus without a look back.

Confession Number Eleven

On Wednesday, Loch followed me again to our second class, this time without his dazzling duo (who I noticed weren't in class either so they probably weren't computer majors just fans of his which made me shake my head) then he once again followed as we walked to our third class.

I tried approaching him after our last class but he walked out with several guys so I didn't want to bother him. I know. I was chickenshit. But Wednesday night I decided I'd let things go too long, not to mention the guilt was killing me, so I thought it best to send him a friendly text. You know, break the ice a bit then I'd ask if I could call him where I'd finally get around to apologizing. That was the plan anyway.

Text Message—Wed, Aug. 20, 10:34 p.m.

Me: Hi

Of course, he didn't answer.

Text Message—Wed, Aug. 20 10:45 p.m.

Me: Can I call you?

He still wasn't answering, but I'd known I'd have to work at it.

Text Message—Wed, Aug. 20, 10:57 p.m.

Me: I wanted to talk to you to tell you how sorry I am for what I did

When he still hadn't answered more than twenty minutes later, I gave up.

Text Message—Wed, Aug. 20, 11:26 p.m.

Me: Okay. I know you're still mad and you have every right to be. Just know that I'm going to keep texting you until you answer… and I've been told that I'm very persistent so there's your warning. I guess I'll try again later. Bye…

So there it was.

He wasn't talking to me because I'm sure he hated me or at best was finished with me, so all I could do was keep trying to contact him, maybe catch him on a good day and he'd let me do my thing.

But what did it really matter? He'd already moved on anyway, first with the woman the night he'd called me drunk saying I should've been there instead of her, then Monday with his pair of groveling groupies.

I lay there a little frustrated. Okay, a lot frustrated because I needed to do this. I had to tell him what an ass I'd been. Then I felt like an even bigger ass because I knew that part of the reason I wanted to apologize was so that I'd feel better about myself.

By Friday morning, my nerves were a bit frayed. I'd texted Loch again on Thursday but he still wasn't answering and I was feeling even worse.

"I'm a bitch," I mumbled as I walked into the kitchen.

Marcy looked sleepily up at me from her cereal bowl and raised an eyebrow.

"I've been texting Loch trying to see when's a good time to call him but he won't answer. And that makes me feel worse about what I did and now I hate myself. If I could just apologize and get it over with, I'd feel better." I cut a bagel in two and put the pieces in the toaster.

"You're doing it again."

I turned and looked at her.

"You're letting him make you feel bad about yourself again. God, Sim, you're a grown woman. Why do you let him get you all riled up?" She spooned some cereal in her mouth as she looked at me, elbow on the table, her head resting in her hand.

"You're right." I frowned. "You're right! Shit! Why do I even care what he thinks?"

I saw her roll her eyes. "Because you like him. Hell, by this point you might even be in love with him since you've held a torch for him since you were five."

This made me sputter. "Wh-what? I'm not in love with him! That's, that's utterly ridiculous!"

"Uh huh," she muttered skeptically as she continued eating.

"I'm not!"

She pinned me with her eyes. "Then why *do* you care so much?"

"He's someone I grew up with!"

"I grew up with lots of guys but haven't contacted them in years."

"Well, I had a crush on him!"

"And he was a jerk to you."

"We were kids!"

"He's someone who hurt you so badly you withdrew for years."

"We were twelve!" I yelled.

"And yet you still care."

I spun around to scowl at the toaster angry at myself for getting so, well, angry.

"Sim…"

I kept my back to her as I buttered both pieces of bagel.

"There's nothing wrong with the way you feel about him."

"Don't try to psychoanalyze me, Marce," I snapped as I got the juice out of the fridge and poured myself a glass.

"I'm not. I'm saying this as your best friend. You and Loch always had something special. I remember being jealous when we were in elementary school because you always sought him out during recess. You liked playing with him more than you did me."

I went to the table and sat, keeping my eyes from hers.

"Even when you weren't really friends in middle school, I still saw how he looked at you."

My head shot up. "What?"

She nodded. "I didn't tell you because he was always such a jerk to everyone and I didn't want to get your hopes up, but when you weren't looking, I saw him." She shook her head. "I sound like the worst best friend ever. First, I don't tell you that then I make a plan for you to get revenge on him. I'm a dick."

I snorted. "You're not a dick. You were just looking out for me." I paused as I thought about what she'd said really wanting it to be true. "Did he really look at me?"

She nodded. "Ryker also told you Loch felt bad about what he did at the dance, right?"

"Yeah."

"And now Loch has that *Little Prince* tattoo…" I glanced at her as she gazed into her cereal bowl then her head came up. "He loves you too," she whispered. Then she looked up at me and said louder, "He loves you!"

Well, my best friend had officially lost it. And I didn't hesitate to tell her this.

"No! He got it permanently inked onto his fucking skin! Don't you see? He's loved you this whole time! He might not know it yet, but he does!"

"Marce, you know how the carpenter's house is the worst on the block? Needs the most repairs? Or the dishwasher has dirty dishes in his sink?"

She stared at me.

"You're wanting to be a psychologist or psychiatrist or whatever yet your brain's fried. I think you need to work on you because what you're saying makes no sense."

She scrunched up her face. "It makes perfect sense! He's felt bad for years. Wanted the opportunity to make things right with you. Then you were right there in front of him and he didn't even know it. Now shit's all screwed up and he feels like a dumbass for not realizing it was you! Boom! Got 'em!"

I rolled my eyes. That was the most ludicrous thing I'd ever heard.

"So now that I've diagnosed the problem, you'll just need to keep after him until his eyes are opened to the truth." She shrugged like it was that easy.

"Diagnosed the problem," I scoffed. "So, is there a timeline on this?"

"I'll bet you're already wearing him down. I'll even bet he'll talk to you today."

"Whatever."

"Let me know." She spooned a last bite into her mouth. "Oh! Party tomorrow night at one of Adam's friends' houses. You're going. Supposed to be some big bash I heard. The guy's an athlete so there'll be lots of hotties for us to check out."

"Uh, thanks for *asking* me to the party. How do you know I'm not busy?"

She was nice enough not to laugh at that. "Do you work tomorrow?" she asked as she got up to take her bowl to the sink.

"Until nine."

"Good. Adam and I'll wait for you here and you can follow us over." As she walked by me, she leaned down and wrapped her arms around my neck giving me a hug from behind. "I'm really sorry I started all this Triple C shit. It was dumb. I was blinded by your hurt and my hurt. I'll try to be a better friend." She kissed my cheek then went to her room to get ready for class.

As I ate my bagels, I thought about everything she'd said and came to the conclusion that studying the mind and behavior had driven my roommate nuts but I still loved her. When I finished eating, I swiped the crumbs from my hands, put my glass in the dishwasher then went to get ready for class.

~*~*~*~

After class started, I noticed that Loch wasn't there. It wasn't that I'd looked around for him, I just knew. And how I knew, I had no idea, and that bothered me which gave me a brief panic attack as I wondered if that meant I was in love with him. Then I chuckled to myself at how stupid I was being which made Cute Guy's Feed Me a Cheeseburger girlfriend look at me disapprovingly. I gave her the biggest smile back and chuckled some more at her disgusted eye roll before she looked away.

When Dr. Lykins released us, I couldn't tell if I was disappointed or happy that I wouldn't be followed by Loch today. Guess I'd find out. I grabbed my bag then made my way outside the building and began my trek across the quad.

When I passed the fountain, I giggled along as I watched a group of girls throwing pennies into it because they were coming up with some outrageous wishes.

"I wish that I ace my government exam!"

"I wish I'd get down to a size four!"

"I wish the clothes manufacturers get their size labels mixed up so I can just *say* I'm a size four!"

Massive giggles.

"I wish the guy I hooked up with over summer finally calls me!"

"I wish my ex's new girlfriend gets herpes!"

Cackles and screams of laughter galore from the girls now and several people around me laughed as we all made our way to our next class or to the student center or wherever everyone happened to be headed.

When I got to Noble Hall I went up the steps and inside only to find myself amidst a small crowd that I found out later was protesting one of the professors not being rehired. I ended up running into a guy who came to an abrupt stop right in front of me which shot me backward where I smacked right into someone else.

"Oh, God, I'm so sor—" I started to say as I looked over my shoulder only to see it was Loch I'd crashed into. Ack! And damn it. The black-rimmed glasses he was wearing made him look hotter than ever.

My eyes were huge as he smirked down at me and it was then I felt his hands on my hips pulling me back into him. He leaned down to my ear and said, "No need to apologize, sweetheart. Your heart-shaped ass near my dick? Pure heaven, *Simone*." Then he let me go and pushed his way through the crowd leaving me standing there frowning.

Ah, so this was how he was going to play it. The jerk was back.

This I could deal with. *This* didn't make me feel nearly as guilty for what I'd planned to do to him.

And *this* made me want to slap his face off.

I made my own way through the crowd and walked inside the classroom heading to my normal seat, sure that a look of pure annoyance covered my face. After class started, I took my notes ignoring the feeling that I was being stared at while at the same time tossing around in my head what Loch had said.

He'd meant it to be condescending and demeaning. He was also trying to show me that I meant nothing to him. I'd just been some girl he'd basically fondled.

Well, two could play that game.

I'd grown up with a big brother who'd given me the brush-off all the time so I had experience. Well, only on the receiving end but how hard could it be?

I only had one thing to say about this: Let's get ready to frickin' rumble.

Confession Number Twelve

I'd soon learn how hard it was acting callously cruel toward Loch. I just didn't have it in me to be mean right to someone's face. No, the only way I could do that was to go behind their back plotting with my roommate. Ergh.

Right before class ended, the professor gave us an assignment that was due that evening (a Friday!) covering assembly language and protocol layers. We had to go to the library to work on what he'd set up, so leaving class amidst groans from people wanting to have their Friday night free—people who actually had lives unlike myself—I made my way to the library to get started.

I went to a carrel next to the window and pulled up the assignment. It was just after noon and I was hoping this would take no longer than the three hours the professor had told us it would. I mean, I wanted to complete it so I could have my Friday evening off too even though my plans were probably to go home, pull up some sappy movie on Netflix, eat a bunch of crap I shouldn't then pass out amidst wrappers of said crap. Go me.

Almost three hours later, I'd just finished submitting my work when a message popped up on my computer.

To: Student.9571589

Student.9551524 (8/22 3:08 PM): Like your heart-shaped ass in those jeans. Especially liked it pressed against me earlier...

What in the world? I stared at my computer screen for a moment while my brain switched from assignment mode to social media mode. And after reading the message, my face got heated as I'm sure it turned a brilliant red.

I looked over my left shoulder to see if Loch was anywhere nearby and when I didn't see him, I stood to look over my carrel. Hm. He was nowhere in sight. I sat back down and decided I'd play his little game right back as I conjured up my inner raunchy phone sex operator (who also might be fairly sarcastic).

To: Student.9551524

Student.9571589 (8/22 3:11 PM): Yeah? Well, feeling your hard shaft against it really turned me on... or was that a sock?

My face was burning now. And also, Big Fat Yikes! I hoped the university wasn't monitoring messages too closely because going before a peer review board in a discipline hearing wasn't my idea of a good time.

To: Student.9571589

Student.9551524 (8/22 3:13 PM): That was all me, baby... and you're more than welcome to come check for yourself

To: Student.9551524

Student.9571589 (8/22 3:13 PM): Am I now? Hm. Just might have to make that happen...

Huh. I was pretty good at this! I have to admit that for a split second I actually contemplated joining the ranks as a supplier of phonic fornication.

To: Student.9571589

Student.9551524 (8/22 3:13 PM): Oh, it's gonna happen... you just need to name the time and place

There was the cocky SOB I knew him to be. What a player. He'd already moved on but was still hitting on me.

To: Student.9551524

Student.9571589 (8/22 3:14 PM): How about right here, right now?

Totally calling his bluff.

To: Student.9571589

Student.9551524 (8/22 3:14 PM): I like the way you think. Meet me in the periodicals room where they keep the old microfiche in five. Doubt anyone ever goes in there...

Cripes! So much for bluffing.

To: Student.9551524

Student.9571589 (8/22 3:15 PM): What, scared to be in the stacks?

No way would he take this dare.

To: Student.9571589

Student.9551524 (8/22 3:15 PM): That a dare?

To: Student.9551524

Student.9571589 (8/22 3:15 PM): If that's how you wanna take it

He'd be backing out in 3... 2... 1...

To: Student.9571589

Student.9551524 (8/22 3:08 PM): The girl's got guts. Okay, meet me in the back corner near Library Science... I'll be waiting...

Holy shite!

He was supposed to back out!

I'd gotten so caught up in playing my role and so confident that he'd bail that when I read his last message I almost fell out of my chair. So now I had a decision to make. Was I really going to do this?

Yes. Yes, I was.

But not for what he thought would be happening. I was merely going to go back there so I could finally apologize and get this shit off my chest. Then I'd walk away, this time for good and not take one look back.

I logged out of the computer then grabbing my bag, stood thinking I'd see Loch smirking at me before he turned and walked out the front door leaving me to be humiliated at his handiwork yet again. But he wasn't anywhere to be seen. Staring pensively out the windows, another thought hit me and I knew exactly what he was planning. I'd get where he'd told me to meet him and he wouldn't be there, reject me, and once again, make me feel like a fool. I just hoped he hadn't brought an audience.

I probably should've just left and gone home, but I was tired of being a chickenshit all the time when it came to him, so I knew I *had* to go to the stacks just to show I wasn't afraid anymore, if only to prove it to myself. Breathing in through my nose and letting it out, I headed to the back corner, preparing myself for gloom and doom which was okay. At least I wasn't backing down.

I got to the section he'd told me to go to and walked between two tall stacks lined with dusty books that looked like they hadn't been touched in years. It was so quiet in this area as if the rest of the library had forgotten its existence leaving it to wither over time. I rounded one large shelf and as I figured, Loch wasn't there. I swallowed roughly just then realizing how tense I'd been, but then I rolled my eyes and turned to make my way back to the front because who was the chickenshit now, when suddenly I was jerked back by a hand that grabbed my upper arm.

"Hey!" I hissed.

"Shh!" he hissed right back.

And seeing him up close again after our naughty repartee was too much. I dropped my bag then threw my body into his slamming him against the wall, and going up on my toes, smashed my mouth to his hard.

I think I must've shocked him because we stayed that way for a moment, me totally molesting him as I climbed him like a friggin' tree, all the while thrusting my tongue into his mouth and whimpering at the feel of his tongue (hesitantly) tangling with mine. Then without warning, he presently regained his senses and the next thing I knew, he'd turned us to where *I* was now backed against the wall, *his* body pressed into me, *his* tongue seeking mine which made me moan loudly.

And now my arms were above my head where he held my wrists in one hand, his mouth still crushing mine and I felt his hand move under my shirt and up under my bra to cup my breast. Oh, my.

My body started undulating against him as I arched my back, pushing my breast forward into his hand wanting more. Needing more. And he gave it to me, rolling his thumb roughly over my nipple then pinching it between his thumb and finger making me gasp into his mouth.

Tearing his lips away but still holding my wrists above my head, his golden eyes burned with heat into mine as I felt his hand leave my breast and slip down over my abdomen to the waistband of my jeans where his fingers slipped teasingly inside a few inches. He let my wrists go but grabbed one again when my arms dropped, and leading my hand to the front of his jeans, pushed my palm into the hardness behind his fly.

"All me, baby," he muttered, his eyes now full of haughtiness as he rubbed my hand over his very hard and very large bulge that I'd implied was a sock.

This made a husky groan escape my throat because I was instantly soaking wet for him. Wow.

"You want me," he muttered, a totally arrogant look on his beautiful face but I couldn't find it in me to protest because he was so friggin' right.

His mouth crashed down on mine again and I felt his hand at my waistband flatten against my stomach before he slipped it down inside my panties. When his fingers glided through my folds and over my clitoris, I wrenched my mouth from his, throwing my head back against the wall and letting out a loud moan.

"Christ," he ground out then his mouth was back on mine attempting to keep me quiet.

But when he slid a finger inside me, there was no silencing me as I ripped my mouth away and said breathily but kind of loudly, "Oh, my God!"

He brought the hand that'd been holding mine against his hardness up and clapped it over my mouth where I panted roughly against it. "Baby, gotta keep it down," he whispered as he pushed another finger inside while his thumb pressed in, moving in circles.

God!

God!

And I was there. I swear, my eyes rolled back in my head as it fell against the wall and I came hard, my body locking tightly, my muscles simultaneously jerking with spasms as I screamed into his hand.

"Fucking hell, Simone," he whisper-hissed and when I opened my eyes and gazed back at him, I saw a look of awe mixed with raw hunger and need on his face. He dropped his hand from my mouth and wrapped his arm around my waist, his hand going down to cup my bottom.

Still breathing hard, I watched as he slipped his hand from inside my jeans then brought it to his mouth and while keeping his intense gold eyes on mine pushed his fingers inside his mouth slowly then proceeded to suck my juices from them. This caused an aftershock to slam through me making me gasp as my legs buckled. His hand on my butt tightened, keeping me standing and now I was the one looking at him in awe.

Holy Jesus.

Eyes still burning into mine, he pulled his fingers from his mouth, having sucked them clean, and laced his other arm around me where both his hands were on my butt, pulling me tightly against him where I felt he was still hard.

"So…" he began, his eyes now dancing with amusement. "I've given you a week to get your head on straight."

Wait, what?

I blinked. Then I blinked again. Then once more for good measure. Was he serious? "You've given me a week?" I whispered looking up at him with a frown.

He nodded while giving me an arrogant look then said, "Thought you needed the time to figure some things out."

Was he serious right now? This whole time I'd been fretting and feeling like crap and he was just giving me time? My frown became a scowl. "*I* needed time to figure things out but you were seeing other women in the meantime?" At his confused look I raised an eyebrow then educated him. "Oh, you know, the drunken phone call I received at midnight when you had another woman with you telling you to hang up? And don't forget the Olsen twins on Wednesday who were hanging all over you. Now that was fun!" I narrowed my eyes at him when he chuckled.

"Babe." When I didn't reply (because how the heck *do* you reply to that?) he stated, "The night I was drunk, that was Nikki, one of Ryker's friends. She was on the couch, I was on the floor and she wanted me to shut up so she could sleep." I looked up at him skeptically before he continued. "Wednesday, that was Laura and Tasha and they're just friends. They knew about you so guess they were trying to make you jealous, make you open your eyes and, in Tasha's words, 'want me back.'" He rubbed a hand over the back of his neck when he told me this, looking embarrassed. Then he cupped my chin and watched his thumb as it glided over my bottom lip. "I haven't been with anyone this week. Been too tangled up in you," he muttered, his eyes moving up, intense on mine. Then I saw one side of his mouth tip up a little which made my eyes narrow even more.

But what he'd said was good news. At least he'd been as messed up as I'd been over everything. Then I frowned. "I've texted you but you haven't answered," I accused.

"Givin' you time," he informed me again with a shrug. "Now what is it you needed to say to me?" It was now my turn to be embarrassed that he knew I wanted to apologize for my stupid plan but I was also getting pissed thinking that all week he'd left me to assume he hated me. He began again, prompting, "Like maybe tell me you're sorry for acting like a bitch?"

Whoa, whoa, whoa. Now, wait a minute.

"Did you just call me a bitch?" I tried pulling away but he held tight.

"I said 'acting like a bitch.' Big difference."

"Not really!" I retorted getting myself in a snit.

"C'mon, baby, you've been the one keeping us from moving forward."

My mouth now fell open. Was he serious right now?

"Babe, I should be whispering sweet nothings in your ear right now making you feel good." He leaned in and nipped at my ear lobe.

Pushing him back I snapped, "Well, if that's your idea of pillow talk then you know nothing about how to make a woman feel good."

I saw his lips twitch. "Seems I just did a pretty fucking good job of making you feel good."

"You have got to be kidding me," I returned and putting my hands to his chest, shoved him again and miraculously he let me go.

"What?" He chuckled which made me even angrier. And when he crossed his arms and leaned his shoulder against the wall as if he were waiting for my apology, this, for some reason, just infuriated me.

"You think you're getting anything from me now, you're sadly mistaken!" I bit out, turning to go.

"Oh, I think I'll be getting lots more from you, sweetheart."

I swung my head around and fired back, "Don't hold your breath," then I snatched up my bag and stomped off hearing him still chuckling as I went. As I headed toward the doors, I wondered how I'd gone from having the best orgasm of my life to being pissed off as all get out.

And there was only one answer to that: Loch Powers who was still as big a jerk as he'd ever been.

~*~*~*~

When I got home I headed straight to the fridge, pulled my container of Half Baked from the freezer, grabbed a spoon then headed to my room where I flopped down on the bed. Sitting against the wall, knees up and thinking about what had just gone down, by heaping spoonful numero quatro, I realized I may have overreacted just a bit.

But Loch had embarrassed the hell out of me which had put me on the defensive, so technically it was his fault I'd stomped off in a huff. Yep, we'll just stick with that theory.

Oh. And that other thing? Where I'd let him make me come in the library? In public? In the middle of the day? Gah! Just what the hell had I been thinking? Anyone could've seen us. God, it seemed when it came to Loch Powers, my brain just went full stupid.

I hung my forearms over my knees and buried my face against an arm letting out a groan.

I heard my door open then Marcy called, "What's going on?"

Keeping my face hidden, I let out a breath. "Loch just gave me the best orgasm I've ever had… in the library."

"Wait, what?" I felt the bed sink as she sat down. "You have to tell me everything!"

I let out a frustrated sigh then sat up against the wall crossing my feet at the ankles.

Looking sheepishly at her, I explained. "I was finishing an assignment and he messaged me on the computer. We got all flirty then he told me to meet him in the Library Science section. When I got there, I thought he'd chickened out but then he grabbed me and, well, I practically jumped on him, we made out, he got me off, we argued and I left."

"Holy shit! That's hot!" She grabbed the ice cream out of my hand and took a bite. Then she frowned at me. "You argued? About what?"

"You know how I've been freaking out this whole time wanting to apologize to him and he wouldn't answer my texts? Well, he told me he was giving me a week to 'get my head on straight' before talking to me. Then he basically called me a bitch and I stomped off."

"He called you a bitch?" Her eyes narrowed, ever on the looking for "Loch the jerk" to materialize again.

"Sort of." At her confused look I explained what he'd said. "Then he acted so cocky the entire time I wanted to smack him." She started laughing. "What's so funny?"

"You." When I narrowed my eyes at her she explained. "You're so into him you can't even think straight."

"Psh! I don't know about being into him." She raised her eyebrows. "Okay, I'm into him. But I've been so out of it this past week. The guilt was about to eat me alive. And now he pulls this?"

"Pulled what? Gave you time to get your head sorted when it came to the two of you? Then flirted with you with an instant message? Then told you to meet him, where he made out with you all hot and heavy not to mention giving you a spectacular orgasm? Yeah, I'd hate it if Adam pulled that on me." She gave me her *get real* look.

"Oh." When she put it like that…

"Yeah. I think he's giving you another chance, Sim. You sure you wanna screw it up? Again?"

"I feel like I've got mental whiplash." I scrubbed my hands over my eyes then looked at her. "What're you doing tonight?" I gave her my saddest face, puppy dog eyes included, letting her know I hoped we could spend some time together.

She chuckled setting the Half Baked on my nightstand. "Nothing. Adam's at some frat thing so it's you and me, babe."

I tackled her with a hug. "Thank God! I need some bestie time!"

We made homemade pizza then caught up on some shows we'd DVR'd, the whole time talking and laughing about random stuff and it was exactly what I needed.

~*~*~*~

"You look different, Scimitar," Thorne pointed out when I got to work Saturday. "You get a haircut?"

"Uh, no," I answered lowering my brow at him.

"Hm." He checked me out more closely. "You get a new facewash?"

I went behind the counter and opened the register to count the money. Looking over at him I replied, "No." My boss was so weird sometimes.

More staring from him which made me a bit uncomfortable.

When I finished counting, I turned to him and snapped, "What?"

Then he nodded and smirked as if he'd figured something out which made me frown. Griffin came up right then, his face immediately mirroring Thorne's. Crap! Did they know?

"Agony!" Griffin declared in a Jamaican accent, nodding and smirking even bigger.

"Oh, yeah!" Thorne agreed with a nod then they fist bumped both making an explosion noise as they wiggled their fingers when they pulled their hands away. Lord.

I bit my lip as I stood there, afraid to ask what the heck "Agony" meant but then my curiosity got the best of me.

"What does that mean?" I asked, looking back and forth between them.

"It means you got you some, girl!" Thorne literally yelled making everybody in the store look at me inquisitively, including the creepy forty'ish gamer guy who always flirted with me.

Dear God.

I mumbled that I was going to open boxes and turning toward the back, got the heck out of there. Thank goodness there were several boxes that needed opening and bills on Thorne's desk that needed tending to which kept me occupied for an hour until it was time for him and Griff to leave.

Don't get me wrong. I was elated that Loch and I had, well, you know, which hopefully meant we were headed for a reconciliation, but the fact that my bosses knew I'd participated in some steaminess was a whole other story. Gross.

But along with being happy, I was also hesitant when it came to moving forward with Loch since I'd screwed things up before, so I wasn't going to get too excited about it.

"Keep on keepin' on, little *goodaz*," Griff said to me when I came out of the office and passed him and Thorne in the hallway on their way out. I saw him give Thorne another fist bump, explosion sounds, finger wiggles and all, and then they left.

I shook my head at how truly strange they were then went back out to the front where I knew Vegas would be since I'd heard him come in a few minutes before.

"'Sup, Sim?" he inquired when I joined him behind the counter.

As I sat on the stool, I shrugged. "Not much. Anything new with you?"

He was looking through a stack of games that he'd pulled out of the return box and shot me a grin.

"What?" I asked. I saw his face get red and blotchy with embarrassment. "What is it, V?"

"Asked Annica to be my girl last night."

Aw! How cute was he!

"Good for you! I'm really happy for you," I remarked leaning over to give his back a pat. "You'll have to bring her by sometime so I can meet her."

His smile was so big it lit up his entire face. "I will."

He caught me up on all that'd been going on with them since last weekend, telling me she'd loved *From Here to Eternity* and had rewarded him with a couple hickies afterward. I'd laughed and teased, "Kids," which had made him chuckle. He told me they'd changed their schedules at school so they had three classes together but he walked her to all the others too. They had the same lunch period so that was covered too. He didn't come right out and say it but he hinted that he thought she may be "the one." This made me smile but I had to remind him that they were only eighteen.

"Look at *Romeo and Juliet*," he countered.

"True. Let's just make sure your story turns out way less dramatic, though," I said with a shoulder bump.

We restocked the shelves and straightened then one of V's buddies came in and they played some new game while I cleaned the windows. Before I knew it, it was nine and time to close up.

"What're you doing tonight?" I questioned as we walked outside to the parking lot.

"There's some Italian restaurant Annica's been wanting to eat at. Nothing fancy but we're goin' there then we're gonna hang with some friends. What about you?"

"Going with Marcy and Adam to some party at one of his friend's houses. Thinkin' after the week I've had I might just get trashed." I shook my head and rolled my eyes to stress that it'd been a really crappy week.

"You drivin'?"

"Yeah…"

"Then no getting trashed," he semi-scolded, eyebrow up.

"Yes, Dad," I answered with an eye roll.

"So you gonna call your guy?"

I hadn't told him the particulars about Loch and my tryst yesterday but he knew we'd talked. "Wouldn't call him my guy. I mean, I'd like for him to be but I don't know if he really wants the same. If he doesn't, we can just be friends but that'd kinda suck, but if that's all we could be, then I'd take it. You know, because I do really like him, I'm just not sure if he feels the same as I do."

V laughed at my jabbering. "He's your guy."

I frowned.

"Just wait and see, Sim. Wouldn't be surprised that if you don't make the call tonight, he will."

"We'll see," I muttered as I opened the Jeep's door.

"Remember. No drinking and driving." He gave me a pointed look.

"I know. Same goes for you. You and Annica have fun."

We got in our cars and left the lot and just as I pulled out, my phone rang so without looking at the screen, I Bluetoothed it answering, "Yeah?"

"You over your tantrum yet?"

Loch. Frack!

"I did *not* throw a tantrum," was my curt reply.

"You did."

"I did not!"

"You so did."

"Oh, my God! That was not a tantrum!"

"S'pose you're not throwing one now either."

This gave me pause because I kind of was. Of course, I had to argue. "No!"

I heard him chuckle before asking, "So what're you doing?"

"Just got off work and headed home. Then going to a party with my roommate and her boyfriend," I snipped, still behaving like a brat but kind of pissed that he'd laughed at me.

"You know where?" he asked.

"No. She just said it was at a friend of her boyfriend's."

"Text me the address when you find out, okay?"

"Why?" I knew why but I just wanted to hear him say it.

"Wanna see you tonight."

I felt a thrill run through me at the thought of seeing him again. "Oh," I whispered having no argument with that.

"And, babe?"

Oh my, how I loved him calling me that. "Yeah?"

"Wanna see *all* of you tonight."

The dip in my womb almost made me let out a moan. Good grief. Just the words from him and I automatically fell to pieces. Jeez.

Still whispering, I answered, "Okay, Loch," because I wanted that too.

"Good. Text me."

"'Kay."

"And make sure to adjust that attitude."

This snapped me out of the haze he'd put me in just seconds before. "You're joking."

"Nope." I could hear the humor in his voice.

"Do you just like pissing me off?" I bit out.

"You're cute when you're pissed."

"You're sick."

He laughed before saying, "Later, baby," and hung up.

And I loved him calling me that too.

I bit my lip hoping this meant we were on the right track but still ticked at how annoying he was.

But all annoyances aside, I shivered because I was looking forward to showing him all of me.

Confession Number Thirteen

"I'm hurrying!" I shouted from the bathroom as I finished putting on lip gloss.

I'd gotten home and practically made a beeline to my room to get ready. Marcy and Adam had been on the couch watching some dude movie between bouts of making out, so it wasn't like they were putting pressure on me. I just wanted to get the evening started so I could see Loch.

Twenty minutes later I was ready, hair down and curled, makeup dramatic. I was wearing my very short and very destroyed denim skirt with a white, flouncy chiffon halter top that buttoned at the neck in the back but hung down so that my back could be seen if I bent over or someone grabbed both sides and held them out. Since I had boobs, I wore my prettiest, white lace bra under it because no way was I letting the girls just hang out on their own. Lastly, I slipped on the cute black wedge sandals with an ankle strap that Marcy loaned me and finally left my room.

"Damn, woman! You look hot!" Marcy said when I walked into the living room.

"Same goes for you! Wow!" She had her dark hair up in a messy bun and I saw she'd redone her makeup after making out with Adam going with smoky eyes and red lipstick that went excellent with her coloring. She was wearing the cute black romper she'd bought a couple weeks ago when we'd gone shopping and had on the black strappy sandal flats she'd gotten the same day.

"Ready?" Adam asked, and Marcy and I nodded as we fetched our purses.

"Oh, what's the address?" I asked Adam as I headed to my Jeep.

"It's over on Andover. Just follow me," he said as he closed Marcy's door then rounded the hood of his Explorer.

I got in my car and quickly texted the street name to Loch telling him I'd let him know the full address when I got there then I followed my friends to the party.

~*~*~*~

It probably wasn't the brightest idea to take two vehicles to the party since there were cars everywhere.

When we got to the neighborhood, we drove by a cute house that Marcy, who was on the phone with me just then, told me was where the party was. I thought, duh, since there were cars parked everywhere nearby and people were mingling in the front yard.

We had to park two blocks down and I texted Loch the address even though he hadn't answered my first text, then we walked back to the house which wasn't too far but I told Adam I was concerned about how many people could fit inside.

"They have a huge backyard. These houses were built back in the eighties when people actually wanted to do shit with their families and wanted yards. Now you're lucky if you get a five by five patch of grass in the back unless you're willing to dish out some serious cash," he informed us.

We walked into the front yard and Adam stopped to talk to a couple guys while Marcy and I hung back checking out everyone.

"Ooohh, that guy's hot," she said, pointing to a tall, blond guy who was pretty built.

"He's okay. I don't usually go for blondes, though," I replied. "But what about that guy?" I nodded my head toward a group of guys talking. "The one in the black shirt?"

"Oh, yeah! He *is* cute! He's got a Theo James thing going on, doesn't he?"

"Once you're finished ogling all the guys, we can go in," Adam said drily having walked back to us.

"Honey, you know you're the hottest guy here! I'm just helping Simone out!" Marcy said with a giggle before tiptoeing up and smacking her lips to his making him grin like a fool.

He took her hand and led her inside the house with me following. Inside, I saw that the living room was packed, the music was blaring and I stayed close behind as Adam led us through the crowd to the kitchen and out the back patio doors to the porch where several kegs were set up. He got Marcy and me a beer then we went farther out into the yard where a bunch of guys were playing beer pong on, you guessed it, a ping pong table.

"Hang on. I'll be back," he said to Marcy and left us to go talk to a group of guys near the fence.

As Marcy and I stood there sipping our beer I remembered why I hated parties where I didn't know anyone because all you did was wait for something to happen. And I'm talking good stuff, not things like drunk guys busting up all kinds of furniture or drunk girls crying because they'd fought with their boyfriend. No, I'm talking stuff like normally shy people singing karaoke, or that one person who goes around telling everyone they love them then when you see them the next day thinking you're pals now they won't even look at you, or the best is watching people dance because we all know that the consumption of alcohol automatically turns you into a backup dancer for Justin Timberlake. Now *that's* the good stuff. And I'd been the star of each one of those scenarios at least once in my lifetime. Yay.

"I've got a doctor's appointment next Tuesday to renew my birth control. What are you on again?" Marcy asked and away we went, discussing all the different methods there were, dying laughing when we brought up the female condom.

"Just... how?" I inquired amidst giggles.

"Hi," I heard from behind me and I saw Marcy's eyes get big.

I looked over my shoulder and there stood Theo James Guy smiling at me.

"Hi," I responded shyly, not really in the mood to meet someone because I was waiting for Loch, but I also didn't want to be rude.

"I'm Troy," he said, holding his hand out.

"Simone," I replied, shaking his hand.

"Beautiful name for a beautiful woman."

Oh, jeez. That was cute but cheesy, but again not wanting to be rude, I felt I needed to answer him.

"Thank you," I mumbled.

"So, you having fun so far?" he asked.

"I'm gonna go see what Adam's doing," Marcy said then walked away before I could beg her with my eyes not to leave me alone.

I looked back at Troy. "Um, what?"

"I asked if you're having fun."

"Oh. Well, we just got here so I'm not really sure yet," I responded with a laugh.

"Wanna go have a seat?" he asked, nodding toward a yard swing that had a canopy.

"Uh, sure," I answered because my shoes and the grass weren't coexisting too well.

Troy and I chatted for a bit and when he saw that my beer was gone, he offered to get us another. When he came back, we talked more and although he really was a nice guy I, of course, was only interested in Loch, keeping an eye out for him. Where was he?

Troy told me next he was from Southern California which was something we had in common so we talked about that for a while. I also found out that he wrestled for Hallervan and was going pre-med which was awesome.

"So what're some cool things to do in Seattle?" he asked, casually putting his arm behind me to rest on the swing back.

Yeesh.

I relaxed, though, because that's all he did so I told him about some of the hot spots in the city that were entertaining. And when he found out I worked at a game store, he was all over that. We talked about some of the games and I told him about beating Vegas but how we were keeping things even so no one would have bragging rights at which we both chuckled.

And that's when I saw Loch standing with a group of guys, cup in hand, laughing and looking at me.

"I've never met a girl who likes video games," Troy said, knocking his knee against mine.

I kept my eyes on Loch who'd looked away, busy chatting up his friends. He had on jeans that hung low on his hips, the muscles of his thighs outlined in them, and a maroon t-shirt that had "Hallervan Bulldogs" in white across the front that was tight enough to highlight his strong pecs underneath. Lord!

But what the heck was going on? Why hadn't he come over? Was he wanting me to come to him? This was just too weird and although I wasn't sure what to do, I was just stubborn enough to wait for him to come to me.

"Well, I wouldn't go so far as to say I like them," I remarked to Troy with a chuckle, still keeping my eye on Loch.

"But you know about them, which is cool," he pointed out.

I shrugged. "Kinda goes with the job." I watched as Loch looked over at me with a smirk then left the group of guys and went to get another beer. I contemplated going to talk to him when Troy interrupted my thoughts.

"That's a pretty awesome job, you have to admit."

Right. Someone was sitting next to me. Talking. And I was expected to reply.

"It's not bad," I agreed distractedly as I watched Loch as he started walking back to his group when a beautiful blond woman came skipping up to him throwing herself against him and lacing her arms around his waist while he held his beer up so as not to spill it. Then he wrapped his other arm around her hugging her to him.

Uh, what.

Troy was saying something but I was too busy focusing on the scene across the yard.

Loch smiled down at the girl who kept her arms around him as she looked up at him saying something which made him throw his head back and laugh. Then my eyes got big when Ryker came out of the house. I was surprised to see him here also and I watched as he gave Loch a head jerk and headed to get himself a beer. But my eyes didn't follow him. No, they stayed on Loch as the woman said something else to him and they both cracked up.

What in the world?

"Simone?" I heard Troy say.

I turned my head to him. "Oh, what?"

"I was wondering if you'd like to go out sometime?"

I glanced back to see Loch keeping his arm around the girl as he turned then they walked inside the house.

"Sorry, Troy. I think I need to go," I announced, preoccupied with what'd been going on, as I stood and started walking toward the house.

"But—" he stood also and followed me a few feet.

But I'd already made up my mind and turned to give him a smile again apologizing as I made my way across the grass to the patio.

Okay, how to handle things. I decided I'd be mature and ask Loch who the woman was. Maybe she was another of his friends trying to make me jealous which was childish and overkill but I didn't think he'd play that card again. From watching the way they'd behaved together, so familiar, flirty and relaxed, I think I already knew. God.

I hated to think the worst right off the bat, but I'd been burned by him too many times—even though a couple times had been in my head but whatever—to think otherwise. So if I found out that she was one of his "friends" as he'd called Ryker's girl, I was going to give him a great big fat piece of my mind then leave, this time making damn good and sure to stick to the plan of never speaking to him again.

My heart was pounding like a bass drum in my chest when I walked inside the house and I was wheezing a bit, finding it hard to breathe. So instead of forging ahead and risking passing out, I turned and went back out on the patio, grabbing a cup of beer off the outside table that a guy at the keg had gotten for himself then I chugged it. At his, "Hey," I apologized, setting the empty cup down and wiping my mouth with the back of my hand then re-entered the house feeling just a smidge better. Glancing around I saw no trace of Loch, so making my way through the throng of party-goers and stepping into the living room, I looked to my left and saw him with Blondie down the hallway that intersected the kitchen and living room. And that's where I headed.

When I got to the entrance of the hallway, breathing suddenly became a thing of the past for me since my heart was now in my throat blocking all my air, because there they were, Loch and the blonde, him holding her chin in his hand as he looked deep into her eyes then he was leaning down getting ready to kiss her and that's when I lost it.

"Loch!" I shrieked loudly making sure I was heard over the music as I stomped toward them.

He turned and the smirk that he slowly gave me was just begging to be slapped right the hell off his face.

"Hey, Simone," he replied, all lazy and casual as if I just hadn't caught him getting ready to kiss another woman, knowing his next step would be taking her into one of the rooms and screwing her.

"Oh! This is Simone!" the blonde said which made me narrow my eyes at her in the most evil way I could manage.

"Yep. This is her," Loch supplied grinning at me, the amusement on his face plainly evident.

And that's when I went full-psycho, completely and utterly going off on him.

"I don't know what kind of bullshit you're trying to pull here, but you're an asshole!" I screeched, hands on my hips as I leaned toward him on the last word.

"I'll, uh, just leave you two alone," Blondie said and slipped out from under Loch's arm going inside the bedroom and closing the door.

Loch kept his amused eyes on me, waiting for me to go on, and I definitely wasn't done. Not by a longshot.

"You know, what I did was fucked up! I know it was. But this?" I put my hand out sweeping it from him to the bedroom door and back several times. "This is worse! If this is your way of getting me back, it's a good one! You sure got me!" I let out a humorless laugh. "Oh, you had me going for a while there but I knew the prick in you would come out at some point if I waited. And you definitely didn't disappoint!"

He smiled bigger and I felt tears stinging the backs of my eyes.

"Yeah, this is all just one big joke to you, isn't it?" My voice broke when I said, "I don't ever wanna see you again! I hate you!" When he snorted at that, I cried again even louder, "I hate you!" and turned to get the hell out of there.

I'd gotten one step away when his arm hooked me around the waist and he yanked me back against him.

"Let me go!" I screamed as tears fell down my cheeks. Shit!

I struggled against him as he led me down the hallway toward the living room. Oh, nice. He was going to kick me out in front of everyone. What an asshole. But as the people parted for us, most of them looking curiously our way, instead of turning toward the front door, Loch kept going straight then down the other hallway. At the end of it, he opened the door to the right and took me inside, closing the door behind us. Then he let me go, which was a mistake on his part, because I instantly turned and reached for the knob to jerk the door open and leave of my own accord since he wasn't going to kick me out.

And that's when I found myself plastered against it, because he'd come in behind me, both his hands on the door over my head slamming it closed. His body was pressed into mine keeping me there and I couldn't take it any longer.

"Let me go!" I yelled through my tears, one hand on the knob the other bunching into a fist that wanted to make contact with his body, particularly his beautiful face.

"Stop," he ordered, one hand coming down encircling my wrist and prying my hand off the doorknob. When I kept grappling for it, he gave my wrist a sharp shake and ground out, "Stop it, Simone!"

And I was done. Putting my forehead against the door, I stammered, "I h-hate you. Let me g-go."

"Baby," he said gently, kissing me on top of my head. "Stop."

"I-I wanna go h-home," I choked out.

"Not happening."

My shoulders slumped in defeat as I wished he'd just get to berating me or humiliating me or whatever he had planned to do to me so I could leave.

For the last time, I lamented, "I hate you, Loch," hoping that by voicing the words, I'd actually convince myself it was true.

Confession Number Fourteen

Loch pulled me away from the door turning me to face him but I kept my eyes down. I couldn't look at him, not after he'd planned on being with that other woman and certainly not wanting to look at all the goodness that was him only to know I'd never have it.

"Hey," he said softly, putting his fingers under my chin trying to raise my head so I'd look at him.

"Just say it," I said, my voice cracking.

"Say what, baby?"

I finally looked at him. Was he really this cruel? This big of a jerk to make me say it?

Yes. Yes, he was.

My whole body shuddered before I said, "Tell me how you led me on to get back at me for what I planned on doing to you then kicking me out in front of everyone." I frowned as I thought about this. "But I guess you changed your mind and want to humiliate me privately first then tell me to leave," I said resignedly, having finally figured him out. I glanced down again, not wanting to get lost in those ochre eyes of his and mistake his look for compassion.

"Simone."

I closed my eyes. "Just get it over with, Loch. Do what you brought me here to do."

I felt his hands cup my face then his thumbs skimmed across my cheeks as they wiped my tears away. Then his lips were on mine and my eyes popped open in surprise.

He pulled away and I saw the sides of his mouth twitch. "That's what I invited you here to do."

I frowned, so confused. "What?"

He smiled sweetly at me.

"B-but what about that other girl? The one who's now waiting for you in the bedroom? The one you were getting ready to kiss?" I started getting mad again remembering it and felt my body go stiff and I took a step back.

"That's Ryker's room. And that was Nikki, Ryke's, uh, friend. She and I, we're buddies. Ryke's kinda bein' a dick tonight, but she's dealt with his shit so much she just laughs it off. She asked me to go with her to his room so she could get a shirt she left a couple nights ago because she didn't want him to catch her in there and think she was planning to leave a horse head in his bed or something. That's what we were laughing about." Now he shot me a look. "And I wasn't getting ready to kiss her. She said her contact was doing something weird and I was looking in her eye to see if I could help."

I stared at him, mouth open as I digested this information totally letting it slide because what he just said hit me. "This is your house?"

"Yep."

Then I forgot to be mad as I looked around at the cozy room with its warm beige walls, a cream and brown comforter on the king-sized bed with matching shams. A well-worn armchair sat in the corner with a small table that had several books on it and a floor lamp to the side. A few framed picture collages of him and his family and some with what I assumed were his friends were hung on the walls along with a colorful geometric print above his bed. "And this is your bedroom?"

"Yep," he repeated.

I took in the dark cherry wood dresser with mirror and matching armoire thinking the room seemed to fit him perfectly, all masculine and dashing. Then I thought of something else.

"But why didn't you come over to me when you saw me outside?"

"Saw you were busy." His eyes suddenly glittered angrily.

"That guy was, um, Trey. I mean Troy! His name is Troy."

"I know who he is."

"He just came up and introduced himself. Then Marcy ditched me and left me with him. I mean, he's a nice guy and all but I wasn't interested. I was waiting for you."

"Wait. Marcy? Belton?"

I nodded. "She's my roommate."

"Christ."

"What?"

He shook his head. "It's all starting to make even more sense."

I waited for him to explain realizing my head was about to explode from all the emotions that'd pinged around in it in the last ten minutes. There was certainly never a dull minute when it came to Loch and me being together. Jeez.

"I'm sure she's filled you in but I was an asshole to her too when we were younger," he clarified. "Lemme guess. You *both* came up with the brilliant plan to get me back, right?"

I bit my lip then nodded dropping my head, eyes on my feet, ashamed at how juvenile I'd behaved. "Sorry."

"It's okay."

My head shot up. "You're not mad?"

He shook his head. "Nah. I deserved it. I was a prick back then."

I looked at him in awe. "I thought you were trying to get me back for it… I thought you really hated me. I mean, I know we had a, uh, moment yesterday, so I was hoping we were okay, but then tonight you were with, um, Nikki and basically ignoring me so I assumed you were back to hating me again."

He shook his head. "I'm still standing here."

"What?" I whispered.

"Still standing here, Simone. I'm not going anywhere unless you want me to."

I shook my head because I didn't want him to go.

Then he continued. "Don't wanna freak you out…" His eyes were on mine as if he was gauging how I was going to react to what he had to say. "But I think I've loved you since I was five."

All the color drained from my face at hearing that. Holy crap!

"Wh-what?" I croaked, my voice all raspy.

He gave me a soft grin that became soft laughter as his hands moved to me, one going behind my neck, the other landing at my waist. "Simone, *The Little Prince* tattoo is for you. I know it sounds cheesy and ridiculous, but when I lost you, it was like my world just fell apart."

"But you hated me when we were in middle school," I whispered.

"Might've acted that way, but you were my best friend. When you moved, it took me a couple years to deal with how I treated you. Felt like shit and I couldn't do anything about it. Mom told me where you were. She had your number, but I thought you'd probably forgotten me so I never called." He rested his forehead against mine. "Do have to admit I was pretty fucking pissed when I finally realized who you were last week."

He was so quiet for several seconds that I was afraid he'd gotten mad again.

"Loch?" I whispered.

"Still standing here, babe."

I loved that. *Loved it.* Loved what his saying it meant.

"I'm really sorry," I said again.

"I know." He pulled away and looked down at me, his smirk coming into play now. "Remember what I told you I wanted tonight?"

And panties instantly soaked. God.

"Yes."

"How about you get to doing what I want?"

I frowned. "You know, you're really bossy, Loch."

"I know what I want," he explained, smirk still at full tilt.

"Well, just becau—"

I didn't get to finish because his mouth came crashing down on mine as he proceeded to give me the hottest kiss I'd ever received. One of his hands snaked its way under my halter top and up to cup my breast, the other moving down and under my skirt where he grabbed my butt then realizing I had on a thong, a purely masculine sound emanated from his chest which was totally sexy.

"Want you, Simone," he muttered against my mouth.

I reached behind my neck and unbuttoned my blouse letting it fall to the floor between us and watched as he took in my lacy bra seeing he was pleased at what he saw.

"Goddamned gorgeous," he whispered before yanking one of the cups down which made me gasp then his mouth was on my breast and he drew my nipple in and sucked hard.

"Loch," I gasped, my head falling back.

His mouth then skated up to the hollow of my throat where he kissed me then on up my neck to my ear where he whispered, "Wanna see all of you, baby."

He moved back, hands on my hips, and gazed down at me as I reached behind to undo my bra letting it fall down my arms then off.

"Fuck me," he mumbled, his voice gravelly with need as he looked at my breasts. Then his honey eyes came to mine. "More."

Keeping my eyes on his, I undid my skirt then pulled it down, shimmying out of it. I now stood before him in my lacy white thong and wedge sandals.

"Fucking stunning," he said his eyes roving up and down my body.

He then turned us, pushing on my shoulders to make me sit on his bed, his eyes still taking all of me in, looking at me as if I was some precious gift he'd received, then he dropped slowly to his knees. He next slid his hands under my bottom moving his body down to where my legs fell over his shoulders, and pulling my hips up, his mouth was suddenly on me and I cried out loudly because, well, *him*.

I fell back onto my hands and watched as he devoured me, completely ravaged me, until his eyes met mine as he continued the deliciousness his mouth was executing and I was done. Completely and thoroughly wrapped up. So full of bliss and contentment in mind and body I'd never known before in my young life that it overwhelmed me and I fell back onto the bed, my hands coming to my forehead in fists as my body responded to what his beautiful and unrelenting mouth was doing to me.

At the same time, I was also scared out of my mind because I knew he was it for me. Knew that I'd been his for as long as he'd been mine and if it went bad it would destroy me. No, obliterate was more like it.

But I couldn't think like that. Wouldn't. He'd told me he was still standing here, which I took as his saying he felt the same way I did. And that was all I needed.

"Oh, my God," I moaned, my voice all throaty and husky as I dug my heels into his back.

Then he did this thing with his tongue and his mouth at the same time, flicking and sucking, and suddenly I was flying, my body lighter than air yet heavy as stone all at once, the duality of climaxing ever baffling.

But I'll just say it was the best freaking orgasm I'd ever had and he'd already given me the first best freaking orgasm I'd ever had yesterday, so how he topped that one was beyond me.

When I was coherent again, I felt his lips moving up. Over my stomach. Between my breasts. To my neck. Under my ear.

"Gonna have scars," I heard him whisper.

I opened my eyes and turned my head, my mouth at his ear and confused, I whispered back, "What?"

He pulled away and looked down at me with a smirky grin. "Buckles, babe." When I still didn't comprehend he added, "Your shoes."

I was instantly all energy as I pushed him out of my way so I could sit up pulling him up with me as I immediately grabbed his t-shirt in the back jerking it up to see if the ankle straps on my shoes had cut him knowing I'd feel awful if they had. What I saw were a few scratches but nothing significant.

With a relieved sigh but barely holding back my laugh, I blurted, "Don't be a baby."

There I was in Loch Powers' bedroom, on his bed naked but for a flimsy thong and I was teasing him. I wanted to die laughing because never in a million years would I have thought this would be happening but I was definitely over the moon that it was.

"Don't be a baby?" I heard him echo and next thing I knew, I was on my back on the bed with him hovering over me, eyebrow raised and I couldn't help the giggle that escaped my throat. He kissed me quick then sat back on his knees grinning and yanked his shirt off and holy cow.

That chest. Those abs. Those tattoos.

I knew my eyes must've gotten big because his grin became a smirk when his hands went to his fly and he unbuttoned his jeans, going up on his knees to pull them and his boxer briefs down and out sprang the most gorgeous, beautiful and *biggest* cock I'd ever seen.

Damn!

"Fuck you hard for teasing, babe," he muttered as he reached over to his bedside table and pulled out a condom.

"Promises, promises," I answered, still staring at his hard length and still teasing not even knowing where this girl was coming from but I liked her.

His eyes came to mine glittering playfully as he put on the condom and I shivered with excitement waiting for what would come next. He reached to my hips and pulled my thong down my legs and off then he was on top of me, his body covering me, the weight of it feeling so delicious, so good it made me moan again.

"Finally gonna fuck my girl and she wants to play," he mumbled, his eyes dancing as he said this. Then I saw them crinkle at the sides when I gasped when the head of his shaft was at my opening. "You ready, baby?"

I'd never been so ready in my life and I nodded enthusiastically which made him chuckle. When he stayed still, not moving, just looking at me, I wrapped my arms around his back, moving my hands down to his butt and pulling him toward me encouraging him to move. Of course he didn't budge, dang it.

"Been waiting for this for a long time, Simone," he said quietly, his eyes intense on mine.

And this made my eyes fill with tears because I'd waited a long time too, I just hadn't known it. I nodded, swallowing roughly and locked eyes with him as he leaned down to touch his mouth to mine.

"Still standing here," he whispered against my lips before thrusting in hard.

"Loch!" I gasped because I was coming again, the anticipation of it all cresting then exploding inside me.

"Fuck. Like that, baby. Feeling your pussy grabbing my cock like it doesn't wanna let it go. Fucking hot," he groaned as his hand went under my thigh and he pulled my leg up to wrap around his lower back. "Gimme more scars, Simone. Dig in, babe."

And I did because, dear Jesus, he felt amazing, so big and thick and hard, literally feeling like he was touching my soul each time he sank inside me. And I loved it.

His lips met mine again before I felt his hands slide under my back and he pulled me up to straddle him and I wrapped my legs around him. Then on his knees, he shuffled us forward to push me against the wall at the head of his bed and that's when the real plundering began (in a very good way) as he slammed up inside me over and over, pumping hard, his eyes never leaving mine.

"Goddamned beautiful," he muttered, his hand moving in between us where his thumb started working me again.

"Loch," I breathed as I felt it building again. Was it even possible to come three times in a row like this?

"Fuck yeah," he groaned. "I feel it, baby." His thumb pressed harder, moving faster.

And I learned it was possible as another climax detonated through my body with the force of a friggin' nuclear bomb at ground zero.

I think I screamed his name, I don't know. My mind was blown by that point. I hadn't even known he'd turned us, my head now at the foot of the bed and I saw he held my leg at the calf, my ankle resting against his shoulder as he continued powering inside, his thrusts long and deep, grinding.

And watching his hips rolling forward and back, his abs bunching and contracting with each drive he made I knew I was witnessing something spectacular, beautiful.

"Keep lookin' at me like that, babe, we'll keep this up all night long," he said between gritted teeth.

"Is that a threat?" I panted.

"It's a fuckin' promise," he replied making me cry out as he drove in powerfully, burying himself to the root on the last word, grinding as he looked down at me as if to back up what he'd said.

His thrusts then became uneven as he searched for his release, but they stayed deep and demanding, fierce, as he pounded in hard.

Then I beheld the most magnificent thing as his body found what it'd been tracking, watching as his abs tightened, his chest muscles became packed, the tendons in his neck strained and he bit his bottom lip planting himself deep inside, grunting as he gave me all of him, the whole while not once moving his eyes from mine.

God.

God!

He came down on top of me, his body still shuddering, his jagged breaths gusting against my neck and I knew. As I held him tightly I knew I'd loved him my whole life too.

Confession Number Fifteen

"I can't," I moaned.

"You can," Loch ordered.

And holy crap, he was right.

I could come again right after he'd made me come once already.

I was riding him, both of us unclothed now, but that had happened while we'd talked.

Earlier, when I'd realized I loved him, my heart had seized and panic had set in and I'd tried moving out from under him, wanting to go home to think on it for an hour or fifty but he'd known and kept me right where I was.

"Don't do this, Simone," he'd warned, pulling back to look down at me.

My breath caught. "Do… what?" I asked, trying to come off as innocent but shocked that he'd picked up on what I was doing.

"Don't leave. You do, you'll just go home and think of all the reasons we shouldn't work. Your crazy head'll bring in past shit that needs to be left where it is. Not lettin' that happen. Your ass is stayin' right here."

I frowned. My crazy head? My ass was staying here? God, how bossy was he? "What if I've got something I need to do? You can't make me stay."

"I can and I will."

"You can't," was my petulant reply. He was still inside me and even though he was only semi-hard, which meant he was now the size of the average man (oh my!), his thrust made my breath hitch.

"Can. And will. Don't test me."

I stared up at him, my mouth open. "You are not to be believed right now!"

"Oh, believe me, baby. I rarely say anything I don't mean."

I pushed at his chest trying to make him move and he chuckled.

"What's so funny?" I bit off.

"When'd you develop this temper? Used to be sweet, easygoing. Now you go off like that." He snapped his fingers at the side of my head.

"Yeah, well, I never encountered a man who tries to tell me what to do *all the time*!" I pushed at his chest again but finally gave up. Jeez.

"It's the red hair, isn't it?"

"My hair's auburn, not red," I shared testily.

"In the sun little pieces that catch it light up like threads of fire. Looks red." He twisted a strand of my hair around a finger examining it.

"You've looked at my hair in the sun?" I asked breathlessly.

He nodded and his eyes came back to mine. "Looked at *you* in the sun, baby. Most beautiful girl I've ever seen. Thought it when we were little. Think it now."

"Loch," I whispered, once again close to tears.

"Yeah. So I'm not lettin' you leave. We've got somethin' here and not gonna let you screw it up. Again."

This made the tears dry up. "How can you be so sweet one moment and a total jerk the next?"

He grinned. "Raw talent, babe." He pulled out then got off the bed hitching his jeans up. "Be back," he informed me then left his room.

I lay there for a moment thinking this was going too fast and then I was up and was collecting my clothes when he walked back in to see me standing there naked, wedge sandals on and clothes clutched to my chest.

"Knew it." He smirked as he stalked toward me, backing me into a wall.

"I-I really need to go."

"Told you. Not happenin', Simone. We've already been through this just the past *week*. I give you even more time to break things down, probably won't see you for a fuckin' year." He tried taking the clothes out of my hands but I held on to them. "Baby. Come lie down with me."

I held my ground then blurted, "What if this doesn't work with us? Huh? What if I give in then we break apart? I'm sure you'll be fine just like you were this whole time. But me? I know what happened the first time you hurt me. I don't think I could take it again."

His eyes narrowed. "What happened the first time?"

Shit.

Shit!

I shook my head. "Nothing. Just let me get dressed then we can talk."

"Not happenin'," he reiterated for the umpteenth time. He suddenly unbuttoned his jeans then down they and his boxer briefs went.

"What're you doing?" I gasped.

"Need to show you I've got nothing to hide and I make no judgments. We're at our most vulnerable when we're naked so here I am, like you. But I want you naked mentally too, baby."

We stared at each other for a moment then I gave in. He led me to the bed, pulling the covers back for me to get in then he followed, turning to face me and throwing his arm over my hip.

"Tell me."

I licked my lips and looked at his chest and when I saw the tattoo over his heart, the one he said he'd gotten because of me, I let him in and told him everything.

"That's why I'm scared," I whispered.

I felt his hand tighten on my hip. "I'm sorry. I had no idea I hurt you that badly. Just please know I've paid for it. Hated myself for a long time. But I promise to give this my all. I want you, Simone. Loved you almost my whole life. I don't wanna lose you now."

And that pretty much sealed the deal. "Okay, Loch. I trust you." And I did.

He leaned in and kissed me which led to some very good things and now here we were.

"Ride me harder, baby," he groaned from underneath me, and who was I not to follow orders. "That's it. Just like that."

He knifed up, grabbing me by the waist pulling me off him then placed me on the bed on my hands and knees entering me powerfully from behind. When he leaned over me, placing one hand flat against the wall then moving the other under me to roll my nipple between his thumb and finger, I cried out as he drove in deeper, panting as I felt my body fire to life.

"Want you to come again," he breathed in my ear.

Frick.

I didn't think I could but this man and his talented everything made it happen and next thing I knew, I found myself cheek to the bed, arms splayed to my sides, completely exhausted.

"I'm there, baby. Still feel your pussy clutching at me. Fuck," he ground out then grabbing my hips to pull me back into him, he sank in as far as he could, burying himself to the hilt and then some as he groaned. This happened two more times with him grunting each time he slammed inside and then he was there.

Good lord.

He fell to the side pulling me with him and I fell across him like a ragdoll. The last thing I remember was him kissing my forehead and telling me to sleep.

~*~*~*~

I awoke to the smell of bacon which everyone knows is the best smell in the world, well, aside from babies. I stretched big then realized Loch wasn't in bed with me.

Duh. He was cooking. I smiled as my hand came to my face, the back of it brushing over one side as I bit my lips thinking about all Loch and I had done last night. After the second time when I'd passed out, I'd awakened hours later to his hard length between my legs from behind as he moved his hips to stroke against my folds. Then I'd turned and taken him in my mouth until he was sated. Then he'd done the same for me and after we'd fallen asleep in each other's arms.

The sun shining through his blinds told me it was later morning, probably eight or nine, so getting out of bed, I found the t-shirt he'd worn last night and pulled it on. Opening the bedroom door I saw the bathroom and dashed across the hall going in to use the facilities. After, I squirted some toothpaste on my finger and "brushed" my teeth then running my fingers through my hair to make it somewhat presentable, I went out and headed to the kitchen

When I got to the living room, I was shocked to see it was already clean from the party. Ryker must've laid down the law or something making people pick up before they left. A yawn escaped as I walked into the kitchen letting myself have another big stretch but when I opened my eyes fully and saw what was going on I froze.

Loch wasn't frying bacon. It was Ryker who was standing at the stovetop doing the honors and he was turned to me and grinning.

Crap!

"Oh. Hey," I blurted staring at him and wondering if I could run back to Loch's room and forget this ever happened.

"'Sup, Simone?" he replied grinning bigger as I tugged at Loch's t-shirt in the front remembering I was completely naked underneath.

"Um, where's Loch?" I asked and just then heard the front door open then close.

"And when you finish with the watering, take the hose around to those bushes on the side of the house."

Holy fuck!

Fuck!

Fuck!

Fuck!

I'll be damned if Ryker's grin didn't get bigger, topping out at shiteating.

Frack!

And I'll be damned if I didn't freeze solid, even more than I had when I'd seen Ryker, topping out at fucking Venus de Milo frozen.

"Hey, baby," Loch said coming into the kitchen and putting an arm around my shoulders then kissing the side of my head.

How the hell was he acting so natural right now?

"And make sure to pull the couch out when you vacuum to get behind it. You know how Ryker likes throwing bags of chips back there and the crumbs get all—Oh! Hi, Simone!" Mrs. Powers said as she came into the kitchen.

Holy holy fuck!

I know I looked like an idiot when I turned to her, my face having frozen as solid as my body, but where my body was just straight up stiff, my face had a look of shock and disbelief and horror all mixed together on it and it was frozen that way. Frozen, I say!

Loch chuckled and gave me a squeeze with his arm around me. "Baby, it's customary to say hi back when being greeted by your elders," he whispered into my ear but loud enough to where everyone could hear it. I knew this because Ryker let out a snort and Mrs. Powers huffed then berated Loch for calling her an elder.

"H-hi, Mrs. Powers." And that was going to have to be good enough because I think my tongue was frozen too.

"C'mere," she said, holding her arms out to me and moving closer. I stepped into her arms and she gave me a huge hug. Then holding my shoulders, she stepped back to look at me. "You're gorgeous, Simone! Look at you! I can't believe you're all grown up! To think I used to change your poopy diapers and wipe your spit-up off my shirts!"

Kill me now.

She gave me another hug squeezing me tightly. "I'm so glad to see you, honey."

And I finally became unstuck and squeezed her back. When she pulled away, I couldn't help the tears that stung my eyes. "I'm so glad to see you too," I said, voice shaky.

"Now, don't you cry! You'll make me cry and I ran out of waterproof mascara and had to use the other kind this morning!"

But that didn't stop the tears that fell as I looked at her which ultimately caused her to cry too in spite of her mascara.

"Loch, bring us some tissues, please," she said, wiping under her eyes with her finger. Loch left me to do what his mom said while she shook her head at me. "I can't believe how time has flown. I mean, I know it's crazy because I've watched my sons grow up but for some reason, inside my head I just kept you little." She chuckled which made me smile as I wiped at my tears too. Then she reached a hand out to mine grabbing it and squeezing, saying quietly, "Your leaving was hard on him, honey. And now you're back. Just what he needed. You're exactly what he needed." She nodded as a few more tears spilled down her cheeks.

And this made me really cry now which was when Loch arrived and handed us the tissues, me using it to dab at my eyes then nose and her wiping away the black that'd left streaks down her face and had pooled under her eyes.

"Mom, you're such a sap," Loch said, and gave her a big hug.

She hugged him back. "I know. Seeing Simone all grown up hit a nerve. I don't know what I'll do when you boys start giving me grandchildren and they start growing up."

When she released him, Loch came back and put his arm around me again. "Isn't she beautiful, Mom?"

Mrs. Powers smiled and nodded. "You were always beautiful, Simone. Even when you thought you weren't. Jacqui and I talked about it a lot, how beautiful our children were. And speaking of, how is your mom?"

Our moms had talked about us. Of course they had. That's what moms did, right? And Mrs. Powers said I'd always been beautiful. I highly doubted the Wednesday Addams years were some of my best, but I appreciated her saying that just the same. Loch gave me another squeeze which I reciprocated.

"She's good. She's teaching in Palo Alto and loves it. Dad's now a Level 68 Partner and loves it too." I smiled thinking about my parents.

"I need to give her a call. Maybe we can get together next summer when she's out of school."

"She'd love that," I answered.

"Well, I need to be on my way. Gotta get by Costco and pick up Cheerios and hotdogs for the kids."

"Drop some hotdogs off here on your way back," Ryker mumbled as he picked the bacon out of the pan with tongs and put the slices on a paper-toweled plate.

"Why? So you can eat the whole package raw and make yourself sick again?" Mrs. Powers rolled her eyes at me.

"No, Ma. I need something easy to make when I come home for lunch. Nuke 'em and it's all good," Ryker explained.

"We'll see, honey," she told him. She looked back at me. "Simone, again, it was so good seeing you. Maybe you can come to dinner with Loch next week? Give me your number and I'll text you."

Loch snorted at this, leaving me to give his mom my number while he walked over to nab a piece of bacon off the plate which Ryker had placed on the table along with a plate of toast and a pan of scrambled eggs.

"Got it. I'll text. You take care, sweetie." She turned to leave then looked back. "And, boys? You make sure to get those chores done." Then she was gone.

I turned to see both Loch and Ryker staring at me. They looked so much alike it was uncanny, the same dark hair, same gold eyes, same build but Loch just had a more polished look about him that I liked. Ryker was just rough. And intense. And scary.

"What?" I asked.

"Mom never likes our chicks," Ryker shared, sitting down and dishing some eggs onto his plate.

"C'mon and eat, babe," Loch said, holding a chair out for me.

"Um, hang on," I said then ran down the hallway to his room, going in and putting on my skirt, bra and thong then putting his t-shirt back on.

When I came back to the kitchen, Ryker muttered, "Fuck."

"What?" I frowned wondering what was going on as I sat down next to Loch.

"He bet you'd come back not wearing my shirt," Loch explained. He looked at his brother. "You got all the chores, dude."

"Fuck off," Ryker mumbled as he bit the corner off a piece of toast.

I looked at Ryker. "Did you make all this by yourself?" Most guys couldn't boil water so this was pretty impressive.

"Yeah, why?" he eyed me suspiciously.

"Nothing. It's just that most guys can't cook," I declared.

"I'm not most guys," he snapped giving me a look.

Yikes.

"Lighten up, bro," Loch warned, shooting his brother a look just as malignant. He looked back at me. "Ryke had to learn to cook. Goes with the sport. He's just bein' a prick now 'cause he's started training already."

Oh yeah, I guess wrestlers did have to be picky about what they ate so they'd make weight for matches, which would lead to their knowing how to cook.

"Sorry, Simone." Ryker glanced at me before stuffing more eggs into his mouth, shocking the hell out of me that he'd apologized. "Fucking starving."

"It's okay," I replied watching him spoon more eggs onto his plate. Maybe that's why he always looked so scary. He was hungry.

"So whaddya wanna do today, baby?" Loch asked.

"I wanna hire someone else to do the fucking chores, *baby*," Ryker answered, giving Loch a smirk and making me giggle to see him behaving so silly.

"Shit's not gonna happen," Loch replied, giving his brother the finger who actively shot it right back at him, then Loch looked at me. "Movie day?"

"Yes!" I squealed. I'd missed movie night when I'd screwed everything up which had made me really sad.

So after cleaning up the kitchen, texting Marcy to let her know I was okay, showering and changing into the clean pair of panties I always kept in my purse (Mom made me do this) but putting back on my skirt and a different shirt of Loch's, helping Ryker vacuum (hoping it'd score me some brownie points with him so he wouldn't snap at me anymore) and after Ryker left to go to the gym, Loch and I finally cuddled together on the couch as he pulled up *Road House* on Netflix and started it.

"Oh, my God, that's Johnny from *Dirty Dancing*!" I shrieked and turned to see the look of distaste on Loch's face. "What?"

"Chick flick."

"So?"

"Babe." He paused the movie and gave me a "get real" look.

"What?"

He leaned in close. "You like my dick?"

I pulled my head back in surprise at his question, my face turning scarlet.

He nodded. "Yeah. Thought you did." He turned the movie back on.

And that was it.

And that made me start giggling looking at Loch sitting there so matter-of-factly as if he'd just explained in great detail what he meant and yet I was still clueless.

He paused the movie again, looking at me as if it had pained him to do so. "What?"

I was still laughing when I said, "I have no idea what you just said."

"Babe." He tilted his head and gave me another look.

And there it was again which made me burst out into more giggles.

"Simone."

I stopped giggling (kind of) enough to ask, "What does that *mean*?"

He sat forward and turned to look at me. "Means I have a dick. You like it. I watch shit like that dancing movie, it means I gotta hand over my dick because I'd no longer be a man." He sat back and restarted the movie.

And now I was dying. I fell onto him choking on my laughter, laughing even harder when I heard him mutter, "The fuck?" When my giggles finally died down, I looked at him (which made me bite my lips to keep from giggling more) and clarified, "That's hysterical."

"Apparently." He raised an eyebrow. "You through?"

"I think," I said with a snort.

"Can we continue?" He waved the remote toward the TV.

"Yes, baby."

He gave a grunt in return and started the movie for the fourth time. But I wasn't finished with him yet. Leaning in, I kissed the side of his neck moving my mouth up to his ear where I lightly took the lobe between my teeth then I whispered, "And just so you know, I happen to *love* your dick."

We didn't finish the movie because I spent the rest of the afternoon proving to him exactly how much I loved it.

Confession Number Sixteen

Everything between Loch and me was going great. I'd never been happier in my life. He was hot, he was a great kisser, he was an even better lover, oh, heck, he was just an amazing guy all the way around. He'd shown me he'd meant it when he'd promised to give me his all and we'd grown much closer. He'd also taken away my fear and now I felt comfortable in our relationship, even exchanging heartfelt I love yous here and there with him. And I did love him to the very depths of my soul. To show him how much, I'd even gone to dinner at his parents' a couple times, his dad had given me a huge bear hug the first time I went which was awesome, then sitting for an hour both times listening to Mr. and Mrs. Powers argue on the dates when Loch had first turned over as a baby or I'd started crawling, things that'd been exciting and sweet to hear at first but just got tedious hearing them repeated. And if that's not showing commitment, I don't know what is. But Loch had also gone with me to Tristan and Sky's for dinner, so he was showing me the same love and commitment right back which was perfect.

But there's always that one thing that tests a relationship and ours was coming up fast.

My birthday was in two days, falling on a Saturday, and although I had to work that night, I was excited because after I got off work, Marcy, Adam, Loch and I were going to a club to celebrate my being twenty-one. What was also exciting was Loch kept telling me he'd gotten me something I'd love but no matter what I did, he wouldn't reveal it to me. And this was driving me nuts.

I mean, I was the kid who, after finding out there was no Santa Claus, made it my mission to know where Mom and Dad hid the presents for Christmas because I had to know what I got. *Had to.* It was an obsession I wasn't proud of. Ugh. So after begging Loch to tell me, I then turned to Marcy who was no help either. Adam refused to get involved and Ryker just laughed at me.

Loch and I had even had an argument over it once and I'd stomped out of his house only to be caught around the waist and hauled back inside as he chuckled while I pouted.

But that wasn't the test. That was just me being a poor sport.

So it was Thursday evening and I was at work. I usually didn't work during the week but Jason, a guy Thorne had hired the week before, couldn't make it, so I'd traded with him and now he was working for me on Sunday which worked out perfectly for my birthday in case I had a hangover.

A little less than an hour before we closed, since we were slow, I was on the phone with Loch.

"You get off at nine?" he asked.

"Yeah. Only fifty-two and a half minutes to go."

He laughed. "Babe."

I was beginning to understand this one-word remark, I think. From what I could tell, it had several meanings, anywhere from his saying it when he was amused, to his using it as a warning, to his muttering it when he thought I was being silly, or to his saying it when he was getting annoyed with me.

Right now he was amused.

"What would you do if the love of your life came in the store in, say, about thirty-forty minutes?"

"A giant Pop-Tart's gonna be coming in?"

"Babe."

Annoyed.

"Wait. Are you gonna surprise me? You know I hate surprises!"

"Yeah, I kinda got that," he said, laughing.

"Are you really gonna come by?"

"Might try. I'm at Dad's garage. They were out having dinner when the alarm went off. Someone threw a rock through the fucking window this time so I swung by to help him and Mom clean shit up. If I have time, I'll come by."

"Okay, baby. Tell your parents I said hi and that I'm sorry about the window. I love you."

"Love you too, Simone. You at my place tonight or am I there?"

"My place. Marcy's staying with Adam so we'll be alone."

"All right, baby. Gotta go. See you in a bit or a little later."

We hung up and I still had forty-six and a half minutes to go so I stayed in the office making Dakota, who was being particularly annoying tonight, stay on the floor in case anyone came in.

A half hour later, I heard the bell jingle on the front door, and thinking Loch had come by, I scooted out of the office to go to the floor just after Dakota had hollered that someone was there to see me. But when I reached the floor, I stopped abruptly when I saw it was Jared, my ex-boyfriend. I'd let him know where I was working in one of the few texts we'd sent each other since I'd moved here and lo and behold, here he was.

"Jared!" I said, going to him to give him a hug.

He bent and picked me up, twirling me around which made me laugh but then his mouth landed hard on mine and he commenced to giving me a long, deep kiss which he tried to make wet too by shoving his tongue in my mouth but I was having none of that nor was I laughing anymore as I tried shoving him away.

"What the hell, Jared?" I sputtered scowling up at him after he set me back on the floor.

"I missed you," he said sheepishly, bringing his hand up and running his fingers lightly over his mouth like he was remembering the kiss. Then he tacked on, "Sorry."

"Well, I miss a lot of people but I don't try cramming my tongue into their mouth. And I have a boyfriend! Jeez!"

"You have a boyfriend?" He looked shocked and hurt all at the same time. "Why haven't you said anything?"

I frowned at him wondering what part of our breaking up he hadn't understood. "We haven't really talked that much lately."

"Yeah, but you could've told me." He looked so hurt and I couldn't figure why. We were broken up for crying out loud!

"I'm sorry. But now you know." I glanced pensively at him. "Did you think... um, did you think you and I might get back together?"

He ran a hand over his forehead and I could tell he was embarrassed. "I guess I thought if you weren't seeing anyone and since I'm not really seeing anyone, that maybe we could hook up this weekend. It's your birthday and I'm staying at my friends' who have a great house with a pool and all and I thought you'd like to come over and celebrate."

I narrowed my eyes. "When you say 'hook up,' are you meaning hang out or something more?"

He shrugged. "Hang out but if you were open to it…"

Wow.

I saw Dakota in the background staring at us as he moved the carpet sweeper back and forth over the same spot which wasn't doing any good. But it reminded me we were closing.

"Well, it's time for us to close, but how about I call you and we can have lunch or something. How long are you here?"

"I fly out Sunday night, so yeah, give me a call." He bent down and kissed me on the cheek this time pulling back to give me a mix between an apologetic and embarrassed grin.

I followed him to the door. "Okay, I will. Bye, Jared." I locked the door behind him and turned to see Dakota staring at me. "What?"

"You're getting all kinds of action these days but you won't give me any of your time?"

I rolled my eyes. "Let's close."

~*~*~*~

I got home around nine-thirty and texted Loch to let him know I was there and that I was going to take a quick shower so to take his time coming over. But when I got out of the shower and checked my phone I saw he hadn't answered so I called him getting his voicemail.

"Hey, baby. I'm home now, so you can come over any time. I love you! See you in a bit."

At ten-thirty when I still hadn't heard from him, I was getting worried so I called him again, and again got his voicemail.

"Loch? Are you okay? Please give me a call when you get this. Love you, baby."

A little after midnight I awoke to find I'd fallen asleep on the couch and immediately grabbed my phone to see if Loch had called but he hadn't. He also hadn't texted. Now I was really worried and called once more.

"Baby. Where are you? I'm getting scared now. Please call when you get this, okay? Love you."

When I didn't hear anything from him in the next fifteen minutes, I risked being cussed out by calling Ryker.

"Yo," he answered.

"Uh, Ryker? Is Loch home? He hasn't answered any of my calls or texts."

"Don't know. I'm not home."

"Oh. Well, if you talk to him, could you ask him to call me, please?"

"Yep."

"Okay, thanks."

"No problem."

What in the world was going on?

Then as I tried coming up with an answer, every horrible thought imaginable bombarded my brain.

Was Loch still at the garage with his parents and something big like a car chassis had fallen on him incapacitating him and now he was at the hospital having emergency surgery and his parents just hadn't thought to call me?

Had the chassis fallen on all three of them to where none of them could call anyone?

Or maybe he'd hit his head on the chassis and lost his memory and his parents were so distraught they'd forgotten to call me.

I hated doing it, but I had to know. So dialing Loch's mom I hoped A) she wasn't stuck under something unable to get to her phone and my calling was making it more frustrating for her or B) all was well, they'd just left the garage and Loch had informed her to let me know if I happened to call her that his phone had died so he couldn't get me.

"Simone? Is everything okay?" Mrs. Powers answered.

She didn't sound like I'd woken her (which was good) or that she'd been trapped under a car chassis (which was even better).

"Hi, Mrs. Powers. Is Loch still at the garage with you?"

"No, honey. We all left there hours ago. Why?"

"Oh. I've been trying to get a hold of him but he's not answering. Did, uh, his phone die and he doesn't have a charging cord maybe?"

"That could be it. You might call Ryker and see if he knows."

"I did but he's not home and doesn't know if Loch's there," I replied, wondering where the heck Loch was. "All right, thank you. I think I'll go by their place and see if he's there and his phone is just dead."

"Okay, hon. If you need me just call. We'll see you later." She was so sweet. And I guess having four boys who'd probably done some pretty crazy things over the years kept her from worrying herself silly over them.

Loch's house was about forty minutes away with traffic, thirty without, and I hated being out on the road by myself this late at night but I was kind of starting to fret now since I'd called him a few more times as I drove.

When I got to his neighborhood, I saw his truck in the drive which scared the bajeebus out of me. What if someone was inside holding him hostage and when he answered the door, he had to give me a code word or something to let me know he needed me to call the police. Ack!

I pulled into the drive and got out, going to the door on shaky legs. It took three rings of the doorbell when suddenly the front door jerked wide open making me jump. But when I saw Loch was okay, I let out a small sob of relief.

"Baby, you scared me!" I said, moving to him and wrapping my arms around him. When I realized he wasn't hugging me back, just standing there stiff as a board, arms as his side, I looked up at him with a frown. "What's wrong?" He took a step forward, pushing me out onto the porch and coming out with me. He closed the door behind him then crossed his arms and looked down at me. He was angry but I didn't know why and it was eerie how much he looked like Ryker just then. "What is it?"

He stared at me, his eyes cold, jaw muscles popping and it was then I noticed that he looked somewhat disheveled, his hair messy as if someone had been running their fingers through it. Then I swear to God, it sounds so fucking cliché, but there was lipstick on his fucking collar.

And all the air was knocked out of me in one fell swoop. Holy shit. But I was able to suck just enough wheezing out, "I-is that lipstick on your shirt?"

He tucked his chin and looked down at it. "Probably." His icy stare hit me again.

What the hell? I looked at him and asked something I was afraid to ask but I did it anyway. "Is someone in there?"

His stare said it all.

"Oh, my God," I whispered as my heart shattered into a billion pieces right there on his front porch. Then for a moment, I felt like I was going to throw up but somehow managed to swallow down the bile that was threatening to make an appearance. The whole time he just stood there watching me, his steely eyes cutting right through me. And that's when the anger finally caught up with me. "There's someone in there with you?" I said loudly staring at him in disbelief.

He smirked and let out a humorless laugh. "How's it feel?" he spit nastily.

My face turned hard as I gritted my teeth. "What the fuck do you mean how does it feel?" I screeched, my fists balling at my sides. "You really wanna know? Well, I'll show you how it fucking feels!" Before I knew what I was doing, I swung my right arm and punched him right in the chin. I was shocked for a beat then I screamed, "*That's* how it fucking feels!" Then I turned and ran to my Jeep wanting to get the hell out of there.

Of course, I didn't make it because I was jerked back by his arm circling my waist and he hauled me kicking and screaming inside the house, slamming the door behind us.

"Let me go!" I screamed, scratching at any part of him I could reach.

He carried me to the couch and threw my ass down on it which gave me more leverage to kick the son of a bitch which I tried my hardest to do but then he grabbed my legs stopping their movement. Putting a knee to the couch, he fell down on top of me keeping my lower half still but then had to grab my wrists, slamming my hands down on the sofa at either side of my head, because now I was trying to punch him again.

"You fuck him, Simone?" he got in my face and cryptically asked.

Upon hearing that, I stopped my assault and frowned up at him wondering what in the hell he was talking about.

"You fuck him?" he now shouted making me jump.

"I have no idea what you're talk—"

"I saw you!"

More screaming and more jumping.

He was so angry.

Then he let go of my wrists, pushed up off the couch and stepped away from me. "Get out."

"I don't know what you're talking about, Loch," I declared looking up at him.

And I guess he'd had enough because he grabbed me by my upper arm jerking me up off the couch and literally dragging me to the front door which he opened and once again ordered, "Get out."

I glared up at him for a beat then I said very low and very dangerous, "You'd better know what the hell you're doing here, Loch, because I walk out this door, we're done."

That gave him pause (finally) then he put his hands in his hair, pulling at it as he started pacing.

"Never been in a serious relationship before, Simone."

I watched confused as he walked then he stopped suddenly, turning his eyes on me. "Never been in love with anyone before."

I frowned at the agony I saw on his face. "I haven't either," I confessed, shaking my head. "You're my first, Loch. My only."

"Then who was the guy?"

I guess I was just dense because I was still clueless. "I don't know who you're talking about, Loch."

He sighed and looked so defeated I took a step toward him but his eyes warned me off. Yikes.

"I saw you tonight. Went by the store after leaving the garage and saw you kissing that guy. Up in his arms. Holding onto him so tightly."

Oh, my dear sweet lord. That's what this was all about? Good grief.

"That was my ex, Jared. He's in tow—"

"Don't give a fuck. Just want you to leave."

"Listen to me, damn it! If you'd shut up for five seconds I could tell you!"

He crossed his arms over his chest and glared at me. "You've got five seconds."

I rolled my eyes. "He's in town visiting some friends. He came by the store to see me. I was gonna give him a simple hug, but he picked me up and spun me then tried kissing me. If you'd stuck around long enough you'd have seen me gripe him out for it. He didn't know I have a boyfriend because I haven't talked to him to tell him! And that's how important that stupid kiss was to me because I've had no idea what you've been talking about for the past twenty minutes!" He squinted his eyes at me as if trying to gauge whether I was telling the truth which made me throw up my hands. "And how about that lipstick on your shirt? Huh?" I pointed a finger at his shirt accusingly.

He looked down at it, perplexed.

"Yeah."

Then he looked up at me and shook his head. "Must've been Mom."

"And I'm just supposed to believe that?"

"It's the truth."

"Maybe you should try believing me then," I shared.

He looked at me in disbelief. "I caught you red-handed though."

I shook my head, fed up. "Jesus. Call me when you realize I'm in love with you and would never do anything like that to you." I looked him right in the eye. "Ever."

I stomped out of his house, getting in my Jeep and going home. As I lay in bed, I thought about how mad he'd been. And I knew Jared and I must've looked bad to him, but it really hurt me that he'd think I'd do that to him. Then again when he'd answered the door, I'd done the same thing to him thinking he had a woman inside.

I sighed. Sometimes it sucked being young and immature.

Just as I was drifting off, I got a text.

Text Message—Fri, Sept. 12, 2:18 a.m.

Loch: Still standing here. I'm sorry. Open your door.

I got up and ran to the front door, throwing it open and jumping right into his arms.

"I'm so sorry," I said against his neck, breathing in his smell that I thought I'd die without. "I thought you had someone over. I should've trusted you. I'm so, so sorry." And cue the tears.

He carried me inside, turning to lock the door behind him then walked to my room where he sat on the edge of my bed holding me as I cried.

"Baby, it's my fault," he said. At my tearful, "No, it isn't," he nodded and repeated, "It's my fault. I should've trusted you. It just hurt like a fucking bitch to see you with him like that. I should've gone in and found out what was going on instead of assuming. Or at least gone in and kicked the shit out of him. That would've made me feel better." He chuckled. "But I guess I was in shock and that's why I reacted the way I did."

I pulled back to look at him, sniffling. "We're quite the pair, huh?"

He nodded, lips pursed.

"This is our first fight. Well, not our first, I guess. I was so stupid at the beginning with Marcy and my plan, cancelling movie night. So I guess that was a fight, huh?"

He shrugged.

"Oh, and then when we were in the library and I left you there." My stomach fluttered at the memory of what had happened before I'd gotten mad and left. "That was our second fight. So this was our third." My eyes got big. "That's three fights in less than a month, Loch. How're we gonna make it? Crap!"

I felt him shaking against me as he laughed. He cupped my face and used his thumb to wipe away my tears. "When we're old and gray I hope we're still fighting like this."

I jerked my head back looking at him like he was nuts.

He smiled, pushing a lock of hair behind my ear. "Means we care, babe. If we didn't, there'd be nothing to fight for."

Oh. Well, that made sense. "Well, I love you and care about you a lot so I guess we've got a lot of fights to look forward to," I informed him.

He chuckled. "I love you and care about you a lot too, so yeah, we do."

"I guess this is good news?" I queried.

He nodded and brushed his lips against mine. "It is. But the best news of all?"

I raised my eyebrows waiting for him to tell me.

"Is all the fabulous fucking makeup sex we'll be having."

I let out a surprised laugh and then he kissed me, long and hard and deep and wet.

And then he got us started on our road to all the fabulous fucking makeup sex we'd be having for the rest of our lives.

Epilogue

Being in love with someone is easy.

Staying that way is easier when you know you're with the one person in the entire fucking world you're meant to be with.

Simone was my person.

I'd loved her since I was a kid, before I even knew what love was. And when she left, I felt an emptiness I'd never known before. And at some level I knew I'd screwed up.

I'd like to say that during the years I spent without her I was a mess and so lost that I could barely find my way but I can't. I was just a kid trying to make his way to adulthood. Hell, I still am, but back then, like I said, I had no idea how to love someone or what love even was.

But having her back in my life has shown me exactly what love is. It might be small things, like me giving her my last jelly bean or her rubbing my shoulders when I'm sore from lifting weights. But it can be bigger things too, like holding her when she cries, telling her it'll be okay, or not talking at all if that's what she needs. It can be her telling me how awesome I still am when I've missed the shot at the buzzer to lose the game on my intramural basketball team or her giving me space when I'm pissed that the Giants lost. Or maybe it's the birthday present I gave to her which was an 11" X 16" picture of us as babies sleeping in the same crib, my arm thrown across her back already protecting her even though I was only nine months old.

Look, I realize it's a miracle that she ever came back into my life but believe me when I say I'll do anything and everything in my power to keep her here and make her happy. I know she knows this too by the looks I sometimes catch her giving me. And those looks are special, they're for us alone and I like it that way because it's as if we have an inside joke with one another. But the joke is on everyone else because they don't get how into each other we are.

Oh, through the years, I know we'll have fights, maybe even some knockdown drag-outs that last for days but I actually look forward to them. Not just for the makeup sex, which of course will always be spectacular, but I know that as long as we're fighting, that means we know we've still got something worth fighting for.

And for however long that is, no matter if it's fifteen years or fifty years, you can bet I'll still be standing here.

Look for Ryker (The Powers That Be, Book 4) coming December 30, 2015!

Check out other titles by Harper Bentley:

The Powers That Be series:

Gable (The Powers That Be Book 1)

Zeke (The Powers That Be Book 2)

CEP series:

Being Chased (CEP #1)

Unbreakable Hearts (CEP #2)

Under the Gun (CEP #3) coming March 2016!

Serenity Point series:

Bigger Than the Sky (Serenity Point Book 1)

Always and Forever (Serenity Point Book 2)

True Love series:

Discovering Us (True Love #1)

Finding Us (True Love #2)

Finally Us (True Love Book 3)

True Love: The Trilogy: The Complete Boxed Set

http://harperbentleywrites.com/

Acknowledgments

To my ladies, Franca, Mel & Sam, I can't thank you enough for everything you do for me. I know I say it every time but I mean it from the bottom of my heart! I love you guys! Forever and a day!

To the Hellbenders, you guys rock my world! Thank you for all the support and love you give me on the daily ;) You're the best! <3

Anne Mercier, you're crazy, you're amazing, you're crazy amazing! As busy as you are, you always have time for me to bounce ideas off you & that's 'cause you rock hard! And thanks for understanding when I get way too excited when our tweets get favorited :P

TC Matson, I love our phone calls that always end up in giggles. You never fail to make me smile especially when supplying me with sounds bites of Mini Man. We're marketing that & making kabillions soon. Lobe you! ;)

Dawn Stanton, your constant support is so appreciated! Can't wait until November when it's my turn :)

To the many bloggers who've spread the word about my books, thank you x a zillion. Know that you are appreciated GOBS!

And to the readers, this is all for you. Thank you <3

About the author:

USA Today Best Selling author Harper Bentley writes about hot alpha males who love hard. She's taught high school English for 23 years, and although she's managed to maintain her sanity regardless of her career choice, jumping into the world of publishing her own books goes to show that she might be closer to the ledge than was previously thought.

After traveling the nation in her younger years as a military brat, having lived in Alaska, Washington State and California, she now resides in Oklahoma with her teenage daughter, two dogs and one cat, happily writing stories that she hopes her readers will enjoy.

You can contact her at harperbentleywrites@gmail.com, at harperbentleywrites.com, on Facebook or on Twitter @HarperBentley

Printed in Great Britain
by Amazon